Charles Eugene McKee

Student's short-hand dictation manual

Devoted to choice selections of literature relating to all the different departments

Charles Eugene McKee

Student's short-hand dictation manual
Devoted to choice selections of literature relating to all the different departments

ISBN/EAN: 9783337204846

Printed in Europe, USA, Canada, Australia, Japan

Cover: Foto ©Andreas Hilbeck / pixelio.de

More available books at **www.hansebooks.com**

STUDENT'S SHORT-HAND

DICTATION MANUAL

DEVOTED TO

CHOICE SELECTIONS OF LITERATURE RELATING TO ALL THE
DIFFERENT DEPARTMENTS OF PRACTICAL EVERY-DAY
LIFE IN WHICH THE SHORT-HAND WRITER
IS LIKELY TO BE ENGAGED.

for the Use of Students

IN

SHORT-HAND COLLEGES, BUSINESS OFFICES,

AND IN

HOME STUDY.

BY

CHARLES EUGENE McKEE,

BUFFALO, N. Y.

AUTHOR OF "THE NEW RAPID" SHORT-HAND, "THE NEW METHOD" OF
TEACHING PENMANSHIP, "THE NEW RAPID SYSTEM" OF WRITING,
"THE STENOGRAPHER'S SHORT-HAND VOCABULARY," ETC.

PUBLISHED BY THE
McKEE PUBLISHING HOUSE.
1890.

PRESS OF
BIGELOW PRINTING AND PUBLISHING CO.,
BUFFALO, N. Y.

PREFACE.

The present work has been long needed in the schools of stenography, and at the home of the self-learner of the useful and beautiful art of short-hand writing.

It is well understood that after the theory of short-hand has been thoroughly acquired it is necessary for the learner to practice considerably from dictation, and especially on matter relating to the subject about to be engaged in, before he can write easily and rapidly, and be fit to offer his services as a short-hand writer. In order to insure rapid advancement it is necessary that the practice matter be of the most practical nature and the lessons carefully graded. It is with a view of furnishing the student with the choicest class of practical literature for stenographic practice that the present work has been prepared.

Teachers and self-learners have long felt the need of a complete work devoted to the various subjects upon which the short-hand student is likely to be engaged. Especially is this true in large and well organized schools where there are various classes in dictation and where many students are fitting themselves for some particular position in the shortest possible time.

The matter presented in the following pages has been very carefully selected, having been gathered during the past three years while the author was engaged in teaching short-hand.

It has been the constant aim of the author to present only matter of the most practical nature, extending over a large field of thought, in many modes of expression.

These lessons contain a large number of practical words and phrases relating to the various departments of business as well as trades and professions, which will acquaint the short-hand writer with all the expressions with which he is likely to meet. It is quite safe to say that the writer who goes through this book intelligently will be able to take from dictation matter relating to any subject at a speed equal to that acquired in the different departments which this work represents.

The dictation matter has been arranged in the form of lessons, so that the learner will have a definite amount of practice work for daily use and not make the common error of writing over a vast amount of work at a time, thus neglecting to gain speed and the ability to read his notes fluently. The object in dividing the work into lessons is also for the purpose of inducing the student to thoroughly study a definite portion of reading matter before attempting to write it from dictation, and thus knowing beforehand the correct outlines for every word and phrase.

A very novel and practical feature of this book is the presentation of a full court trial, so arranged that a real case can be conducted in the school room, thus giving the pupil a thorough and practical drill on the various steps in a case, as well as practice in short-hand writing from real court proceedings. This course of procedure is not only extremely interesting to the student, but it acquaints him with court work in a practical form, and enables him in a very short time to be complete master of all the technicalities of the work.

This book is sent forth with the hope that it will be the means of assisting short-hand writers of all systems in their efforts to acquire a complete mastery of swift writing, and that it will also prove highly beneficial to teachers of phonography in supplying the students in their charge with good wholesome material for stenographic practice.

TABLE OF CONTENTS.

TO THE STUDENT.

In entering upon your practice of short-hand from dictation you should resolve to make a careful study of each lesson before attempting to write it. While you may be able to outline nearly every word correctly without previous study, yet there are numerous expressions that are peculiar to the line of work in which they occur that should always be written in a connected, and sometimes contracted, manner, and unless you give the lesson careful study beforehand you will fail to get the good from this practice that might otherwise be obtained.

It requires constant vigilance and study during the student's early practice to master the art of short-hand, so that he can write easily, rapidly and legibly on all subjects.

After this book has been written through once it will be well to practice mostly on that matter given in the book relating to the line of work in which you expect to engage.

Each hundred words for some distance in the following lessons is shown by two perpendicular strokes, appearing thus: ‖. The headings of articles have in no case been counted, but in the business letters the salutation and closing are numbered with the body of the letters.

Amounts expressed in figures are generally counted according to the number of words used to express them, rather than the number of figures used, thus: 245 is counted as *four* words, two hundred forty-five, *not three* words, one for each figure.

LESSON I.

THE WAR THAT MADE US FREE.

In Words of One Syllable.

For a time all were at peace; but at last a war broke out that took more time, and cost more men, than all the wars of the past. You have heard of it, it may be, by the name of the Revolution.

There are some old men, who fought in that war, who are alive this day. You see the cause of this war came out of what our men thought to be their wrongs. They thought the rule of England too hard, and that they should have their own men to rule them. They would have gone on as they were, if they had thought that England was just to them; but she put a tax on the things they had to use. She had a large debt to, pay, and so she thought it fair our men should help to pay it; and our men held that they ought to have a voice as to what the tax should be, and fix what they knew to be right.

Do you know what a tax means? It meant, in this case, that when our men bought a thing, they had to pay a few cents more than its real price, and these few cents were to go to England. Of course, these few cents from all sides grew to be a good sum, and was quite a help. England, at this time, made a law which we know by the name of the "Stamp Act." This law, which gave to England a

time the tea was set on fire.   All this made our men more
and more set in their own way; and the King grew in a
rage with them. He made some strong laws, sent troops
to Boston, and put in force a bill called a Port Bill,
which would not let a boat go in or out the port, save
that it brought food or wood.   One of their own men
stood up and said this was a "bill to make us slaves."
And the wood and food had to be brought in a new route,
and not straight in the bay. Not a stick of wood or a
pound of flour could be brought in a row boat, or straight
in from a near point; it must all go round to the place
where the English saw fit, where they could stop it and
see just what was there.

Of course this was hard for the people of Boston, and
they did not bear their wrongs in peace.   They had gifts
sent them by land—of grain and salt fish and sheep.
From the South came flour and rice, and some times gold
for the poor.   So that the Port Bill made all feel to them
like friends, for all towns took up the cause of Boston as
their own.

This was just what the wise men at the court of King
George had said would be the case.   They knew it would
make our people more strong to drive them with hard laws
to fight.   And so it came to pass, as the two great men,
Burke and Fox, had said.   King George was set in his way,
and would not change, but did his best to push the laws
through.   The Boston Port Bill was one of the things that
made the States one.   For they had but one mind on these
harsh laws, and stood as one man for the right.   The day
when this Port Bill was first put in force the Town Hall

in one of the towns was hung with black, as for a death; the bill was on it and the toll of bells was heard all day.

If we could have stood in Boston in those days, we would have seen that there was not much work, and no ships at the wharves but those of England. There were guns in view, and men with red coats in the streets. There were tents on the green, and clubs that met each night to talk of this strange turn in things, and what was best to do. They did not want war, but saw no way to get out of it. Great men spoke of it here and there, and each speech was read at the clubs.

"We must fight," grew to be the cry. But there were some, of course, who felt sad at all this, who thought it wrong not to do the will of the King in all things. They said this land would come to grief, for we were the ones who had the most to lose by war. These men had the name of "Tories," and the rest did not look on them as friends, but held them as foes. Some of these men went back to their old homes, and came here in the troops of the King to fight their old friends. Some did not go, and came round to new views, and took part in the wars that came to pass in time. All knew that the ranks of the King would be made of men who had fought in wars, and were known to be brave; while on our side they would be raw men, who did not know the art of war. But still our men were brave, and they said, with strong hearts: "The strife may be long, but the end is sure. We will fight for our homes, for our lands, for the right. We will be free." (1,634.)

LESSON II.

AN ADDRESS TO THE YOUNG.

Of course every young person, whether a young boy
or girl, a young man or a young lady, has to think very
much of the future. We are looking out to the future;
we think sometimes how many years it will be before we
have reached the ripe old age of four-score years, and the
young man looks at time, measured in that way, as a very
long space, that it will be a great while before the course
will be traversed, that there will be an abundance of
opportunity to do a thousand and one things, that there
is much time ahead, that it does not matter if I squander
my time here and there, there are so many days, weeks,
months and years ahead of us, what matters it if I do not
make the best use of the fleeting moments. Youth is the
time for pleasure and recreation. I am not here to say
anything against all reasonable amount of recreation, play
and out-door exercise. I believe that it is our duty to
engage in these things. There is a time for all things, a
time to go to bed and a time to arise; there is a time for
play and recreation; and we must have all these things if
we would live rightly.

A young man starts out into life with a certain amount
of capital, so to speak; we will call it capital—we mean
the plans by which a young man can make headway in

the world; these are his opportunities; take away these and one of the important factors that make up his success in life will be gone. God has given you certain faculties, to some one talent, to others two, three and four, to each one enough necessary to achieve success in life. God gave you time—time to improve. We can accomplish nothing without time. Now what is time? Time is our opportunity, time is money. I have had a sign printed which is hanging up in my office (I think there are the same in many offices), reading, "Time is Money." That was a hint, of course, to persons who wished to take up my time with something that was trifling or of no special importance.

Now what is the first proposition? One of the first propositions I would make is this: That you do at once that duty that devolves upon you at this time; do not put off until to-morrow the duty which should be performed to-day. This habit of procrastination is one of the many causes for the failure of young men. To be sure that the duty will be performed, you must do it to-day.

We can only make an impression in some one direction; we can only attain excellence in some one thing. The same man can not be a great lawyer, a great theologian, a great statesman, a great scientist. It is impossible that one man can be all of these.

To accomplish anything there must be system; system in work, system in study; no man can accomplish anything in practical life without system. System requires that you must not attempt too many things at one time. It may be well enough to make a few suggestions. You are here for the purpose of acquiring a commercial education, to keep books in a regular business manner, to do those things that business men are required to do; and to do them well you must work with a vim and a will.

There is another thing that I would call your attention to, and that is, do not expect help, do not ask for it, do not permit anybody else to do for you what you ought to do for yourself.

Now time is given to you for the purpose of enabling you to work out your salvation, so to speak. I can not too firmly impress upon you, young as you are, that this is of great value, that time is too precious to be thrown away, that it is your duty to so divide up and use the time allotted to you as to enable you best to accomplish the important part that you have in life; you want to begin now. There are often seen pictures of "Old Father Time," and how does he look? Why he is bald behind, and has a lock of hair in front. Now what does that signify? Did you ever think of it? I will tell you, my friends, what it means. It means that you must seize the forelock, and the forelock is so placed that you may seize it. In a moment Time passes by; his forelock is out of reach and only the bald skull, which you can not seize hold of, is before you. Now this is the idea you must have in mind, time is going on; several minutes have gone since I came in this morning. We can seize Time by the forelock, but when he is past he is gone. You can not afford to lose any of those precious moments. So do not waste your time trying to accomplish two, three or four things, when you can accomplish well only one; that would be only a waste of time. Think of these things and search out the difficulty in the way. Such is the condition of life; such is the opposition, so to speak, that young men will meet. It will not do for you to throw away your time as I see some young men do. Having made up your mind, and you want to be careful about that, pursue your end with avidity, continually, with system; pursue it with the idea that every moment goes; and then rest assured that success, prosperity, happiness and usefulness will come to each and all. (979.)

THE ACCUMULATION OF HABITS.

"Like flakes of snow that fall unperceived upon the earth, the seemingly unimportant events of life succeed one another. As the snow gathers together, so are our habits formed; no single flake that is added to the pile produces a sensible change; no single action creates, however it may exhibit, a man's character; but as the tempest hurls the avalanche down the mountain and overwhelms the inhabitant and his habitation, so passion, acting upon the elements of mischief which pernicious habits have drawn together by imperceptible accumulation, may overthrow the edifice of truth and virtue."

LESSON III.

DEPARTMENT OF CORRESPONDENCE.

BUFFALO, N. Y., June 12, 1890.

MR. C. B. JENKINS,

Birmingham, Ala.

Dear Sir: In reply to yours of the 10th inst., I am happy to inform you that the person about whom you desire information merits your entire confidence. Of his financial means I am not precisely informed. I fully believe them, however, to be adequate to the requirements of his trade. But of his character and habits I can speak in the highest terms. He is prompt and punctual in all his transactions, and I believe no person ever had occasion to apply to him the second time for the payment of his account.

I am happy to be able to send you these assurances, and, trusting that your business relations may prove mutually profitable and advantageous, I am,

Yours respectfully, (121.)

HOWARD S. PERKINS.

SPRINGFIELD, O., June 12, 1890.

MESSRS. GREEN, JONES & Co.,

New York City.

Gentlemen: The goods ordered by us on the 10th inst. arrived this morning, and we are sorry to say that they are a great disappointment to us, being so inferior to the class of goods we have been handling that we can not offer them to our customers. This is a very busy time with us, and as many customers were waiting for these goods delay causes us great annoyance.

After comparing these goods with our former orders from your house, we have concluded that a mistake has been made by some of your clerks in filling the order. We trust that you will replace the invoice with goods of a superior class at once.

Hoping to hear from you immediately, and in the meantime holding the goods subject to your order, we remain,

Yours very respectfully, (137.)

J. B. CLEMENT.

NEW YORK, March 15, 1890.

MESSRS. A. R. WHEELER & CO.,

105 Market Street, Boston, Mass.

Gentlemen: We beg leave to introduce to you the bearer of this letter, Mr. Henry Hodge, a partner in the highly respectable house of Hodge, Baily & Co., of Boston, who is about to visit your city for the purpose of extending the commercial relations of his house with the principal firms of your place. In recommending our friend to your notice, we particularly request that you will not only forward his interests by your influence and advice, but that you will also make his stay in your city as agreeable as possible. In case Mr. Hodge should need any money, you will oblige us by supplying him with funds, not exceeding one thousand dollars, taking his drafts upon us at three days' sight in reimbursement.

We beg that upon similar, and all other occasions, you will freely command our services, and we remain,

Respectfully yours,   (145.)

WILLARD & CHANNING.

———   •

OFFICE OF THE
CAPITAL CITY COMMERCIAL COLLEGE,
ANNAPOLIS, Md., March 28, 1890.

MR. B. N. WINGFIELD,
                    Amsterdam, N. Y.

Dear Sir: Your esteemed . favor of the 20th inst. was received to-day.   It gives us great pleasure to comply with your request, and send you in to-day's mail circulars and general information relative to our college course.

Since you have already intimated a desire to study the art of short-hand writing, we would respectfully call your attention to the course of study in this department as shown in circulars sent herewith.   We have every facility for giving you a thorough and practical knowledge of this important branch of education.   You are no doubt aware that this is a study which is becoming of more value every day.   The many improved methods that have been adopted by the business world demands young men and women who can take charge of office work and attend to general correspondence.   Never before in the history of the country were so many positions open to those who can write short-hand and operate the type-writer, and there is no field of labor which promises such great returns and immense advantages as does that of stenography and type-writing.   Should you be so engaged at present as to be unable to attend college at once, we can assist you materially by mail before you come here.

Trusting that we may hear from you at your earliest convenience, we remain,

Yours very truly, (229.)

J. R. Holland, *Pres.*

Headquarters of

National Association of Naval Veterans

Philadelphia, June 9.

Capt. A. F. Lee, Secretary Grand Council.

Dear Sir and Comrade: It affords me great pleasure to be able to acknowledge the receipt of your communication of recent date, conveying the pleasing intelligence that the Council would cordially welcome the Naval Veterans on the occasion of our proposed reunion. The amount agreed upon to be appropriated, whatever it may be, will be gratefully appreciated and no doubt used to advantage. The location and surroundings of the quarters assigned to us in the Capital is all that could be desired. The action of your committee reflects credit on the intelligence, patriotism and generosity of your people, who, it seems, have not forgotten the heroic achievements and brilliant exploits of our navy during the late war, and I am fully convinced that it will be the means of bringing into the ranks of the G. A. R. many of our people who are absent without leave. To all the members of the Council I extend sincere thanks, and trust I shall have the pleasure of their personal acquaintance in the near future.

Very truly yours, (176.)

William Simmons, *Commander.*

LESSON IV.

Dear Sir: I regret to say that the person whose name you mention in yours of the 10th inst. is totally unworthy of your confidence. He has no capital, and, what is worse, is wholly destitute of any sense of business or moral obligation. He is well known to have been in financial difficulties for some time past, and contrives to temporarily bolster up his affairs by obtaining new credits, and systematically underselling his goods.

Sooner or later his failure is certain. How long he will stand depends entirely on his ingenuity to disguise matters, and the indulgence and credulity of creditors. In the end, I am convinced his creditors will obtain next to nothing.

I regret that I am obliged to give this account of any brother tradesman; but since you request it of me, and it is highly important to your interests, I ought to speak with ingenuousness. (150)

Dear Sir: We regret very much that your esteemed order was not delivered, and the inconvenience and disappointment caused you thereby. We beg to say that we are in no way responsible for the delay; but that on the contrary, we have used every effort to secure the prompt execution of the order. Unfortunately for us it happens that the manufacturers are overwhelmed with business at the present time and there is no possible remedy. We hope, however, to be able to prevail upon the manufacturers in this particular instance to make a little extra exertion, and have written them a very urgent letter. We feel certain that if our request can be complied with, they will do all that we can desire. As soon as we hear from them will telegraph you the result of our communication, and hope that it will be such information as will be wholly satisfactory.

Regreting the inconvenience to which you have been put, and thanking you for past favors, we remain,

Yours very respectfully, (171.)

Dear Sir: We are in receipt of your esteemed favor of the 14th, and in reply beg to state that the general depression in the shipping trade still continues. Efforts have been made to construct some kind of an organization which would control the freight market by fixing minimum rates, but the interests involved being so numerous it has failed in its object.

For months past ship-owners have been unable to sail their vessels with a reasonable margin of profit, and the depressions have lasted so long that a number of ships have been obliged to succumb, causing many boats to be thrown on the market under forced sales, and disposed of at heavy sacrifices.

Should any sign of improvement arise we will not fail to inform you of it, and beg to assure you that in this as in other matters, your interests will always command our best attention. We are,

Very respectfully yours, (156.)

Sir: On the 18th of July we informed you that we had received from Mr. Henderson a quantity of goods, as per list then inclosed, and that we intended to dispose of them as soon as opportunity offered. Accordingly, when our fall trade commenced, we put them up at auction, and we have now to inclose you the account-sales of the same. Although they net considerably less than their cost, it is by twenty per cent. more than the same goods would now sell for, as you will perceive by a few coats which were omitted in the first sale and sold yesterday. We are extremely sorry to have to render so unsatisfactory an account of sales. As soon as the proceeds are due we will remit you for them, and hope that any further transactions you may intrust to our care will prove more profitable. Business is very bad here; money extremely scarce; and many of our dry-goods merchants have suspended payment. In fact, times were never so bad before; and it appears to be the same through the entire commercial world. By accounts from your side, we learn that prices are uncommonly low, which, no doubt, is the case; and if we have not too many goods sent out in the spring, our markets will probably improve, so as to encourage speculation. We shall always be glad to hear from you, and to know what is the state of your markets.

Yours respectfully,   (248.)

Dear Sir: We are in receipt of your favor of the 14th inst., inclosing order for goods, in respect to which we beg to remind you that you have omitted to furnish us with references, and that you make no mention of the mode in which you propose to pay for goods.

We need scarcely remind you that it is customary in all cases of a first order being given, to furnish satisfactory references or to forward cash, and as we have not heretofore had the pleasure of transacting business with you and have, indeed, no knowledge of you, we must request that you furnish us with the names of some two or three respectable houses with whom you are in the habit of doing business, or to express your willingness to pay ready money for the goods ordered on receipt of invoice.

Trusting you will not consider us unreasonable in our demands, we are,

Yours respectfully, (157.)

My Dear Sir: I received your interesting communication of the 12th, early this morning. I wrote to you about two months ago, but not receiving a reply I concluded that you had changed your place of business, as I had already heard that you contemplated going west early in the fall.

I was very sorry to hear of your misfortune, but am pleased to hear that your loss was largely covered by insurance. I trust it will not be long before you are in your new place of business, and I predict for you greater success than you have ever met with before, for in my estimation you handle the finest class of goods in the market, and I am sure the public will not be long in finding it out. As I did not hear from you, I sent my orders to a New York house, but as the goods ordered from them will soon be exhausted, I shall, as usual, place my orders with you.

(2)

Our business in the past three months has not been as prosperous as it was the same months the previous year, but it is growing better of late and the outlook for the coming year is brighter than ever before.

With best wishes for your future success, and trusting that our business transactions will prove as satisfactory to both parties in the future as in the past, I remain,

Yours respectfully,   (238.)

Dear Sir: In reply to your favor of the 12th instant, I will forward the parcels to you for Mr. Henderson as you request.

With regard to obtaining new business, there is no reason why you should refrain from soliciting or accepting orders for new business from persons not already our customers, which may come in your way in any part of your district.   What we do not expect our agents and canvassers to do is, to interfere with existing connections obtained through another agent.

We do not make allowances for advertisements.   We advertise very largely from this office, and consequently in a systematic manner.   No fixed allowance is made under the head of postage, but while the directors do not object to refund the expense of posting circulars, etc., they expect the amount expended in that way to bear a fair proportion to the amount of business procured.

I will send the supplies which you require, and trust you will be successful in working up a profitable agency in your district.

I am, yours faithfully,   (176.)

LESSON V.

Dear Sir: Your friend, Mr. Ransom, has handed me your account, and asks me to certify the same as correct. This I certainly can not do in its present form, as no deduction has been made for the diminished size of service-pipes and fittings, the deduction for which should have been at least ten per cent.

With regard to the second part of your account, namely: for the replacing of sewers, I observe that in your letter of 25th February last, in answer to my inquiry, you informed me that the cost would be about $2.00 per section. The account you send in makes it just $2.25 per section; and, there being five hundred sections, the difference is a considerable one. I can, of course, understand that, after the slight deviation from the plans agreed upon between us, there may have. been some small amount additional per section over and above the amount estimated, but how you make the price run up twenty-five cents per section I can not understand.

I shall be glad to have a reply at your earliest convenience, stating what deductions you are willing to make, as the other accounts are nearly all settled, and it is desirable that the matter should be closed altogether and handed over to the authorities at an early date.

I am, yours truly, (228.)

Dear Sir: Your esteemed favor of the 1st instant has been duly received and contents noted. I had expected to make you a visit before the first of the year, but matters are in such shape that I find it impossible for me to leave here for some time. I can not make any arrangements now, until things are fixed up in this district, but, when that is done, will see what I can do for you. The report of the year's work will be issued on the 9th of next month. It will give me pleasure to mail you a copy, which you will please examine closely before insuring in any other company. You will find this company as good as any in the United States, and better than most of them in many respects.

Hoping that you will finally decide to give us the preference, I am,   Yours truly,· (151.)

Gentlemen: Having formed an establishment in this place as merchants and general agents, we take the liberty of acquainting you therewith, and solicit the preference of your orders. From our experience in mercantile affairs generally, and our intimate acquaintance with business as conducted in this place in particular, we venture to promise that we shall be enabled to execute any commission with which you may favor us, to your satisfaction, and in the most prompt and economical manner. At least we can safely guarantee that neither zeal nor attention shall be wanting on our part to insure to your friends every advantage that our market may afford; nor will there, we trust, be any deficiency of ability to fulfill their instructions and promote their interests.

Possessed of ample means, not only for the service of our friends, but also for carrying on an extensive export and import trade on our own account, we shall be glad to avail ourselves of any advantage that your market for British products or manufactures may, from time to time, present, by making you consignments. We shall therefore thank you to keep us constantly advised of the state of your market; and as we shall‖be ready to make advances to the extent of two-thirds of the invoice amount of goods consigned to us for sale, on receipt of invoice, bills of lading, and orders for insurance, we shall, on the other hand, expect the same indulgence from our friends and correspondents.

We are extremely desirous of rendering our correspondence mutually advantageous, as the only means of placing it on a solid and permanent basis; and this, be assured, will be our constant aim.

Your faithful servants, (283.)

Dear Friend: The undersigned, employees of the Ohio Columbus Buggy Company, deeply regretting your departure from among us, desire your acceptance of the accompanying memorial, in testimony of our affection and respect for you as a gentleman and a mechanic, and as a faint expression of our appreciation of your kindly efforts to render our connection with this manufactory not only' pleasant and agreeable to ourselves, but profitable to the company.

Deeply regretting that our connection must be severed, we shall gratefully remember our association in the past, and hope always to be held in pleasurable remembrance by you. (99.)—   (Signed by the Employees.)

To the Employees of the Columbus Buggy Co.

Gentlemen : I am in receipt of your kind letter and testimonial. Wherever fortune may cast my lot, I shall never cease to remember the pleasant associations of the past few years, and the many kind attentions I have received at your hands. If our relations and labors have been pleasant, I do not forget that they were largely made so by your always generous efforts and willing co-operation.

I will ever cherish your beautiful gift as a memorial of our pleasant years together, and can only wish that each of you, when occupying positions of trust, may be as warmly supported and as ably assisted by those in your charge as I have been since my connection with yourselves. Thanking you for this testimonial and your generous words of approval, I remain,   (140.)

Dear Sir: Replying to your communication about diseases of the blood, I am happy to give you the most positive assurance of a speedy, perfect, complete and permanent cure.

Some years ago I discovered a method that has enabled me to cure every case I have treated since that time, where my instructions have been obeyed. Since then I have made other discoveries that now enable me to cure such affections much more rapidly than I could formerly.

To permanently cure these disorders, we must not only antidote the poison and eradicate it from the blood but we must repair all the damages it has caused. Unless this is done, the disease is likely to return sooner or later in some form or other. The time required to accomplish all this

varies, necessarily, with the constitution of the sufferer, the
severity of the disease and the damage it has caused. In
the early stages, I usually can effect a cure in a very short
time, but when it has invaded every part of the body and
deranged and impaired the functional powers of the various
vital organs, time is necessary as well as proper treatment.
It is always well, as a precaution, to take the remedies for
some time after all indications of the disease have disappeared, as a guarantee against a relapse. I have cured
cases in six weeks, when they were under my treatment
from the beginning, but the average time is longer, though
the symptoms may all disappear in that time. When
patients have been imperfectly treated or drugged with
improper remedies, I find nearly as much trouble in over-
coming the effects of former medication as in curing the
disease. The effects of such medication often require the
greatest exercise of skill.

Hoping that you may consider this matter favorably
and that I may receive an order for a course of treatment
at an early date, I am,

Very respectfully, (324.)

_____

My Dear Sir: As a teacher of young men and boys for
many years, I have had a laborious and most painful experience in inculcating the thousands of absurdities and
irregularities in English orthography. To stamp on the
memory of youth a jargon imposed on us all by the authority of lexicographers is an undertaking about equally
hateful in the labor, hopeless in the prospect, and stupid
in the accomplishment. The contradictions and enigmas

in spelling are well adapted to beget in bright youths a persuasion that the claim of knowledge, instead of being a series of beautifully connected links,‖is a tissue of tangled knots and kinks. A dull boy never learns to spell; a smart and willing one acquires the art after many years as a hateful conventional necessity.

Your alphabet, which is very agreeable to the eye, can be learned in a few days by any one, and then distinct reading follows in a few days more. I have no doubt a child, ignorant of all letters, could be taught by its use to read slowly but surely in a few weeks, while now such reading is the work of years, and spelling is almost never learned.‖

I must commend your alphabet for its good apppearance. Without meaning to disparage the "Anglo-Saxon," which I now receive, and with high respect for its conductors, I am free to say that the beautiful page of your New Testament is vastly superior to any other phonotypy I have seen.

It is perfectly truthful, but may seem like flattery to say that your intelligent and tireless zeal in advancing this great reform has no parallel so far as I know, and will doubtless be better rewarded by your own conciousness of benevolence and right intention than by any eulogy of‖mine. You will meet with much opposition, be ridiculed by the stupid, the conservative will inveigh against your "mad innovation," the literary bigot will dread the loss of his occupation, but time, perseverance, and the common sense of the world, will effect your triumph.

I am sincerely your affectionate friend,   (350.)

LESSON VI.

My Dear Sir: As to the times, I confess the prospect is dreary. The great manufacturing establishments of our country are stopping or keeping on at a sickly pace. Business seems to be approaching a stand-still, and the different branches of business are relatively like the members of the animal body. If one branch is paralyzed, it affects all the rest. It is not wise to suppose that merchandising and building will go on as usual when the factory, furnace and the machine-shops are stopped. A paralysis in industrial pursuits affects the prices of property, real and personal, and makes the stock which was worth $1,000 under the favorable circumstances not worth more than $500 under the depression.

So far as I have been a silent observer in the legislative hall, and perhaps shall remain silent, unless the tariff question comes up, and I should get an opportunity on that. There is always difficulty to obtain the floor on a question of importance, and I never was good at a scramble for precedence.

As to the political horizon, I scarcely know what to say. The news this morning of a bloody revolution in France raises the curtain to new scenes for the imagination to dwell upon. Where is this to end? To what is it to lead? How is it to affect us? I can not imagine an answer to either of these questions. It may be but a three days' commotion, and it may convulse the whole earth. The war with Mexico I fear, too, is not yet over. It has taught us, I trust, that it is easier to get into a fight than it is to get out of it when you are in.

Sincerely your friend,   (294.)

Dear Sir: You have been referred to us as a super-intendent of public schools, who would very likely be interested in new and improved text-books for schools and colleges.

During the past few years, public attention has been directed to the importance of the subject of the young observing the laws of health, and to meet the popular demand for a text-book suitable for use in common and high schools, we have published the "Eclectic Physiology." The work is entirely new, is richly illustrated with engravings and colored plates, and the subject is presented in language that is ‖simple, direct and within the comprehension of every pupil. We desire to call your attention especially to the subject of alcohol, and its effects on the human system, food, vegetation, prevention of disease, and the invaluable notes and suggestions that follow each chapter, which, in the hands of a faithful teacher, will become a most efficient means of inducing original thought upon the part of the pupil, by leading him to bring to the comprehension and illustration of each subject his own stores of observation and experience. Introduction and sample copy price, 75 cents; exchange price, 50 cents. If you‖contemplate the introduction of some work on this science, we would be pleased to submit a sample copy for your examination.

We also take pleasure in inviting your attention to the "Eclectic Primary History of the United States." Sterner duties will not permit the vast majority of pupils in the public schools to pursue an extended course of historical study, but it seems almost imperative that all should learn the principal facts connected with the origin and growth of the Republic. Some knowledge of history, through the powerful aid of association in memory, is indispensable to the best instruction in║geography. The names of many of the states—Maryland, Virginia, Florida, Georgia—had a historical origin; and Lexington, Yorktown, Fort Sumter, Atlanta, Gettysburg and Richmond are destitute of interest to the pupil who is ignorant of the historical memories that cluster around them. Even if the historical text-book is used only as a reader, each of these studies becomes a most efficient assistant to the other. The "Eclectic Primary History" has more than one hundred illustrations by the best artists. Nearly every page is illustrated. The introduction and sample copy price is 50 cents; exchange price, 30 cents. In║simple and accurate language, judicious selections of topics, clear and perfect type, and wealth and beauty of illustrations, we believe the "Eclectic Primary History" is unsurpassed, and in such belief we submit it to the judgment of educators, and confidently hope for their approval.

Trusting that we may have the pleasure of hearing from you relative to the introduction of one or both of these text-books into your school, we remain,

Yours very respectfully,   (475.)

Dear Sir: Your favor of the 14th received and contents noted. All of our engraving is done by a peculiar process, to the virtues of which we attribute the success we have had in cut-making. The cuts are not made by what is properly known as photo-engraving. They are etched on zinc, a much harder metal than is used in the ordinary process, and as this gives a plate of the maximum hardness the sharpness of line is very apparent in the printing. To make you a single plate of the size you specify, three and one-half║by five inches, would cost two dollars and seventy cents. If you had as many as twenty plates of this kind to be made we could make a special price of two dollars and fifty cents for each plate. As to the electrotype, that would depend largely on the size of the edition. As we have said, these plates being of extra durability will run a large number of impressions—three times as many as an ordinary photo-engraved plate. We never print from electros at all, and some of our plates made in this way have been subjected to║as many as fifty thousand impressions without perceptibly impairing their sharpness. We rather think that one of these plates would be good for one hundred thousand impressions.

The one virtue of having an electrotype is that in case of an accident to any plate you always can replace it instantly. Still, electrotypes, however well made, will not produce precisely as sharp an effect as the original engraving, and every additional electrotype will be a little heavier—not enough to be ordinarily discernible or to do any damage, but still enough so that an expert might be able to detect the difference.║ Electros of plates of this size would cost about fifty-five cents each, if you conclude that you would want to use them.

Now as to the result of the plate, of course you understand that the "stream can never rise above its source."
To get a sharp plate you must have sharp copy, but from
plates of yours that we have seen printed we judge that
you are familiar with this part of the work. As to the
reduction, there is no exact scale for such work that we
should commend as being better than any other scale of
reduction.‖ It is necessary, however, that the matter be
reduced considerably in order to get the sharpness of
effect. The plates as they are printed in the journal that
you admire are four inches wide by a little over six inches
depth, and the original from which they are engraved are
six inches wide by something over nine in depth. Of
course, this proportion holds good as to the space between
the lines and everything else connected with the plate.
The plan that we have found simplest and best in prepar-
ing matter of this kind is to have blanks of the‖dotted
lines printed on them, then the short-hand characters are
drawn in with a pen. It is an exceedingly difficult operation, not to say a tedious one, to put in these dotted lines
uniformly with the pen, and it is much cheaper to have
them printed. We could supply you with these blanks at
a small cost if you wish us to do the work.

By trimming down the margin a little you could make
them conform to the dimensions of your own plates by
the one-third reduction if desired, so that the general
effect of the plate‖as to spacing would be about like ours.

Trusting that we will receive your order, and promis-
ing to do all in our power to give you entire satisfaction,
we remain,   Yours very respectfully,   (633.)

LESSON VII.

ADVERTISING CORRESPONDENCE.

Gentlemen: We send you by this mail a copy of *The American Home Illustrated*, and if you will carefully examine the same, we think you will admit that its typographical appearance, illustrations and literary merits are not exceeded by any household paper in the country. We feel confident that your advertisement in our paper would prove very profitable to you, reaching, as it does, 20,000 homes, being read by the several members of the family, lent to the neighbors and afterwards preserved. If you want to place your goods before all these people, please examine advertising rates inclosed, and ‖ we hope to receive a trial order from you. We also inclose you rates for the *Home*, and several lists of papers, and we particularly ask your attention to our " Bargain List." Kindly look over our rates and compare them with others ; and if we can not save you money, we do not expect your order. Should you favor us with an order, we will strive to work for your best interests.

Awaiting your reply, we are, ·

Respectfully yours, (179.)

Dear Sir: We take pleasure in sending you by mail to-day a copy of the *Illustrated American Home*. Since its beginning in 1884 it has met with marked success, and is now a permanent and well-established journal.

It is about to enter its fifth year of publication, and its subscription list has reached such proportions in this city and county that the publishers have decided to issue, January 1st, in addition to the regular edition, a separate city and county edition (same size and number of pages), especially devoted to the residents of this city and county. In addition to the news of the city, it will have a correspondent in each village in the county. Besides our regular subscription list in the county, we have a carefully-selected list of 2,500 names, to whom we will mail sample copies of our paper.

As we desire to have our city merchants well represented in this county edition, one of our partners will call on you during this week for the purpose of securing your advertising patronage.

With the compliments of the season, we are,

Yours respectfully, (190.)

Dear Sir: I am about putting out some advertising direct from this office, instead of sending it, as I have done previously, through advertising agents.

I would like to make use of your paper, if you can make me a price that will justify me in doing so. I find times very hard and money very close, consequently must ask you to give me your very lowest prices or I can not accept them.

Will you kindly inform me the best possible price you can give me for a one-inch advertisement, to run one year, or a three-inch advertisement, to run one year—taking, of course, the run of your paper, but not to be printed in any stale position all of the time? Please state the circulation that you will guarantee, also what will be your very lowest price for local or reading notices per line, to be used as

I may require. I expect I shall want to run testimonials adapted to your locality as they may develop, for which, of course, cash will be paid whenever the work is done. If your rates are low enough in proportion to the circulation, I will send you electrotypes of the ads. at once, with an agreement for the same, the payments for which I propose to make quarterly.

If you can make any use of the goods described in the *Health Helper*—a copy of which I send you by separate inclosure—I will be pleased to have you do so, and should you find them satisfactory so that they justify you in recommending them for your own use, or that of your friends, or if you can get some druggists to handle them, I will be pleased to cancel the small advertisement I now give you and make a larger one, provided, by this means, I can find a way to pay you promptly for an increase of your space. I would say, in this connection, that I must have such rates as will enable me to make it profitable, or I can not increase or renew my patronage of your paper. I believe the goods I am offering are the best there are in the market, but you will doubtless understand yourself that competition is severe and that it is very difficult to obtain a foot-hold; consequently, at present, I am not able to pay any fancy prices for the advertising I solicit.

I trust that I may be able to use your columns to advantage, and that you will feel a kindly interest in my undertaking, and, should I find your paper paying me, I will be pleased in the near future to make a contract that will be of mutual benefit to us.

Hoping to hear from you at once, I am,

(Dictated.)   Yours truly,   (472.)

Dear Sir : Your postal card was received this morning. We hope you will succeed in obtaining a few subscribers in your city for our new Directory. We are sorry, however, to receive your intimation that you do not think of having your own business announced in our new work in a more extended entry than the one we give gratis, and would ask you to reconsider your decision.

Our Directory will be altogether in advance of anything of the kind yet published, and will no doubt be the standard work for reference for professional and commercial men. We are sure, therefore, it would be a mistake not to allow a notice of your various departments to appear in its pages.

The paragraph in my circular to which you refer means that we intend to include every firm of any importance, and those who do not wish to occupy more space will have the free entry of two or three lines only. We sincerely trust that you will see the great advantage to be derived from a more extended entry, and that we may receive matter for such a notice before the fifteenth of the month.

Over five thousand of the first edition have already been taken, and our subscribers include the heads of the public schools, banks, commission agents, clerks, public bodies, hotels, hospitals and similar institutions throughout the country; just those classes, in fact, amongst whom your departments would be the first to be recognized.

Trusting that we may hear from you on the subject soon, we remain,

Your obedient servants,   (272.)

(3)

LESSON VIII.

INSURANCE CORRESPONDENCE.

Dear Sirs : The subject of life insurance interested me at an early age, and for twenty years past I have given it no little study. Experience has convinced me that for people of small means and for those taking the risks of trade it is the safest and most profitable mode of invest-ment that can be had for the future.

The important question for the consideration of the policy-holder is : "Which is the company whose sol-vency is unquestioned, whose methods of business in the past gives a guarantee that ample provision will be made for the extraordinary exigencies of the future and whose prudent and economical management will afford a reason-ably low rate to the insured?"   After critically examining the claims of the leading companies of the Union, I have given the preference to yours as fully answering the question ; and have allotted to it the largest amount it will insure upon a life. Comparing the terms for many years with many companies, I am satisfied that my preference for yours is justified.   Its conservative methods and care, both in selection of life risks and financial investments, have frequently come under my observation. Your company is taking a leading position amongst the largest companies, and only requires its claims to be pre-sented in new territory to maintain its ascendency. Wish-ing the company the same success in the future that it has enjoyed under your past administration, I am

Very respectfully yours,   (240.)

Gentlemen: I take pleasure in making the statement that I hold policy No. 368, dated December 5, 1848, on my own life in your Insurance Company of Philadelphia, Pa., and that at my suggestion different members of my family have from time to time procured life insurance polices, until now there are in my family five policies on the lives of four persons, which have been running from five to thirty-five years   I am gratified to state that, having had an intimate acquaintance with this Company from its organization, and also its very economical management, its prompt settlement and the payment of its numerous death losses and other claims, impels me to pen these lines, feeling well assured that I shall receive the friendly regard of as many persons as may be induced to take a similar course and procure insurance in your Company.

I have had the pleasure to make collection of numerous life policies, some of them of liberal amounts, and hand the proceeds over for the benefit of the helpless and destitute mothers and children; and I know what it is to observe the gratitude and joy that come from the widow's heart in the hour of destitution and bereavement.

With warm desire for the continued prosperity and success of your most excellent Company, I am,

Very truly yours, (224.)

Gentlemen: It affords me great pleasure to testify to the very satisfactory manner in which the business of your Insurance Company has been conducted. The steady increase of its surplus and the character of its investments speak well for its stability. Its clear and comprehensive reports and the politeness of its officers in promptly answering inquiries that I have occasionally made have been a source of gratification. Should the future management be as successful as the past, the taking of a policy on my life will be one of the best financial investments I ever made. I have kept a careful account of all money paid as premiums, and should I live to an age beyond the time allotted the life-tables, the amount of the policy will far exceed the money paid as premiums, had it been invested at the usual rates of interest at the time of payment ; and further, during all these years I have had the comfort of knowing that a fund was accumulating to aid the loved ones dependent on me for support, had I been taken from them. Congratulating you on your past management, and wishing you continued success, I am,

Most truly yours, etc.,   (200.)

Gentlemen: It gives me pleasure, as a policy-holder in your Company, and one personally acquainted with a number of others, to be able to state that I have yet to hear of a single member who has the slightest cause for dissatisfaction with the business conduct of your Insurance Company. I believe a policy in your Company to be the best safeguard a man can give those dependent upon him, against the loss which would follow his sudden death, and also the safest and wisest method of accumulating the savings of years—much better in my opinion than any savings institution in the country. I have been in the habit of advising all young men to insure their lives in your Company and I shall continue to do so.

Yours sincerely,   (132.)

Gentlemen: I became a policy-holder in your Company thirty years ago, and I have observed the constant and increasing growth of its business and resources with much satisfaction. Its success has been owing to wise and economical management, and it now occupies the foremost rank. Its assets are invested in the best securities. Its losses are promptly paid, while the low rates, resulting from large dividends of surplus, afford the best opportunity to obtain a safe and cheap provision against the uncertainty of life.

Yours truly, (87.)

Gentlemen: The operations of your Insurance Company, being marked with such pre-eminent success, I can not do otherwise than express my unqualified approbation of its management. It is thirty years since I took out my life policy (the one on the endowment plan having matured a few years ago, was promptly paid), during which time I failed to discover anything objectionable or unsatisfactory in its administration. The dividends paid, if I mistake not, are larger than those of any other company. Indeed, so well pleased am I with it in every respect, that I invariably recommend it to the favorable consideration of all my friends who desire to invest in reliable life insurance.

Very respectfully yours, (116.)

LESSON IX.

RAILROAD CORRESPONDENCE.

BALTIMORE, Md., May 1, 1890.

COL. CHARLES MARSHALL.

Dear Sir: I hand you herewith the Belt Railroad ordinance as it passed the City Council. I also call your attention to an amendment proposed by Mr. Smith, of the Second Branch, to be entitled "Section 13," which will be found on page 442 of the Second Branch Journal, under the date of April 28. This amendment, you observe, provides that all property of the Belt Railroad Company, its successors or assigns, shall be forever liable to such rate of taxation as may be placed upon other railroad property and corporations in the State of Maryland and Baltimore City, not now exempt from taxation, and that the sale by the Belt Railroad Company of its property shall not be construed to deprive Baltimore City of its rights conferred by this section.

I also call your attention to an interview had by the committee of the Taxpayers' Association with the Mayor, which you will find in the *Sun* of this morning, in which it was stated by the committee that if the Baltimore & Ohio Railroad Company should purchase the Belt Line Railway then all the property of the Belt Railroad would come under the exemption from‖taxation granted to the Baltimore & Ohio Railroad Company by its charter.

I desire your opinion, therefore, upon the following points:

1.   Would the amendment of Section 13 change in the slightest particular the present rights of the city and of the State of Maryland to tax the Baltimore Belt Railroad Company and its property?   In other words, I wish from you an opinion as to whether the constitution and the laws of the state, as they now are, do not provide for the taxation of the property of the Baltimore Belt Railroad precisely as would be the case if the proposed amendment of Mr. Smith were adopted and attached as a new section to the ordinance.

2.   In case of the sale to the Baltimore & Ohio Railroad Company or other railroad company exempt by its charter from taxation, would the Baltimore Belt Railroad Company's property by such sale become exempt from taxation, or would the city or state lose its right to tax the property?

I would be obliged to you for a prompt opinion in this matter.   Very respectfully,   (380.)

JOHN B. McDONALD.

BALTIMORE, May 1, 1890.

MR. JOHN B. McDONALD.

Dear Sir: Your letter of to-day gives me so little time to prepare an opinion that I must answer your questions briefly and without going into a full statement of the reasons upon which my conclusions are founded.

1.   It is very clear that the Baltimore Belt Railroad Company, having been organized under the general law

of the state, and having no exemption from taxation, all its property and franchises are subject to taxation as now provided, or, as may hereafter be provided, by the laws of the State of Maryland for taxing railroads. All its property and franchises being thus subject to taxation under the constitution and laws of the state as much and as fully as the property of individual citizens is subject, I do not perceive how the amendment offered to the 13th section of the Belt ordinance (page 442 of the Second Branch Journal) could possibly make the road's liability to taxation any greater.

In answer to your first question I am, therefore, of opinion that the constitution and laws of the state now provide for the taxation of the property of the Baltimore Belt Railroad with precisely the same extent of power and right as would be the case if the said proposed amendment were adopted and attached as an additional section to the ordinance, and that the proposed amendment of Section 13 would not change the present rights of the city and of the State of Maryland to tax the property and franchises of the Belt Railroad Company.

2. By Section 22 of the Act of Assembly of Maryland, Chapter 242 of 1876 (the General Railroad Law), it was provided that no railroad company should purchase any railroad constructed by any other railroad company without the authority of an act of Assembly authorizing it. If an act of Assembly should ever be passed authorizing the purchase of the Baltimore Belt Railroad by the Baltimore & Ohio Railroad, and such purchase should be made, I am of opinion that the property of the Balti-

more Belt Railroad would not by such sale become exempt from taxation, nor would the state or the city lose its right to tax the property. Yours truly, (368.)

CHARLES MARSHALL,
PHILADELPHIA GRAIN ELEVATOR CO.

PHILADELPHIA, December 22, 1887.

Dear Sir: In connection with our interview yesterday relative to the refusal of your employees, under the orders of a local labor organization, to deliver to us cars to our pier, we desire to submit—

That the only point at issue is whether your company will tolerate the refusal of certain employees to perform regular, established duties, with the intent to deprive us of our business, unless we shall concede dictatorial power to said labor representatives.

Our explanation of our wages, etc., were parenthetic, and simply given to show you that we were paying our employees full established rates, and our men are satisfied with the same. This is a matter not within your jurisdiction nor proper for discusion with your employees.

We protest against the unlawful attempt to deprive us of our railroad connections, and demand, without delay, the restoration of the same, and will hold your company liable for all resulting loss or damage and amenable as a public carrier for permitting the unlawful obstruction of our rights.

Awaiting your prompt attention, we remain,

Very truly, (178.)
PHILADELPHIA GRAIN ELEVATOR CO.
FRED. W. TAYLOR,
Manager.

A. A. McLEOD, Esq.,
General Manager, etc.

PHILADELPHIA, December 27, 1887.

A. A. McLEOD, General Manager.

Dear Sir: The strike ordered from Port Richmond has developed the fact that many of our old and faithful employees have been compelled by others to join the organization known as the Knights of Labor. While the Reading Railroad Company has never objected to its employees voluntarily connecting themselves with any labor organization they may see fit to join, it will protect them at all hazards and at any cost from being forced into any union where their own wish would be to remain free; and any employee of this company, or of the Coal and Iron Company, guilty of‖using any undue or improper influence upon any of our men to force them to join any society against their free will, will upon proof furnished us, be insantly dismissed from our service and never allowed to return to it; and any employee furnishing such information will be fully protected from any harm by reason thereof. Please give this notice to the General Superintendent, with orders that it be repeated to the head of every department of the Railroad and Coal and Iron Company. (184.)

AUSTIN CORBIN,

President.

LESSON X.

The Philadelphia & Reading R. R. Co.,
    General Office, December 29, 1887.
John H. Davis,
    Pottsville, Pa.

Dear Sir: Your message to me was repeated to Mr. Corbin, President of this company, and I am directed by him to reply as follows:

Positively we have nothing to discuss or arbitrate; the strike was ordered because we discharged men for refusing to perform a duty which the law made incumbent upon us to perform, and for the non-performance of which no reason on earth existed. Our men should have performed it promptly and cheerfully. Not a word of complaint from the first has been made as to the fair, honest treatment of employees, and the time has‖now arrived when any dictation by any one in our employ as to how we shall do our business will be followed by the immediate discharge of the meddler. Employees of this company will be required to decide now whether their first allegiance is to the company that employs and pays them, or the Knights of Labor. If that allegiance is to this company we will stand by them at all hazards and at any cost; if to the Knights of Labor first, such men will not be allowed in our service a minute. (194.)

                    A. A. McLeod.

Philadelphia, February 9, 1888.

Dear Sir: The President of the Philadelphia & Reading Railroad Company has handed me your letter to him of the 7th instant, with the request that I reply to that portion of it relating to the trouble existing between the Philadelphia & Reading Coal and Iron Company and the miners. I assume that you are familiar with the contract made between this company and its miners last September. In violation of its terms, nearly all the employees of the company left its service on the 1st day of January last, and a large number have not returned. There are at‖present working for the company at the mines about three thousand men, and there would be a much larger number at work if the men were left to exercise their own judgment, and were not deterred by threats of personal violence.

We are willing to discuss the question of wages with any person representing the men actually in the service of the company. As we have stated heretofore, if the men had continued at work under that contract after the 1st day of January, and had, at any time thereafter, desired a conference in relation to the matter of wages,‖the officers of the company would have met them, or their representatives, on the subject. If and when the miners return to work a conference upon the question of wages should be desired on their part, we shall be ready to confer with them, with the understanding that no basis different from the one already in existence will be established that will require this company to pay more for labor for the same class of work than is paid by its competitors.

Yours, truly, (284.)

GEORGE KEIM,
President.

MR. JOHN W. HAYES,
  Philadelphia.

The Philadelphia & Reading R. R.
December 29, 1887.

I am directed by Mr. Austin Corbin, President, to issue the following notice to the employees:

" To such of our old employees as have stood manfully and faithfully by us, we feel obliged and thankful, and shall not forget them. But the time has now arrived when all our employees will be required to decide whether they expect to retain their places by reason of honest and faithful service and prompt obedience to the orders of the company that employs them and pays them, or by blind obedience to the direction of the Knights of Labor, through which organization the‖leaders hope to coerce us into the employment of men who consider their first obedience due to that order.

"The men who stand by us will have employment, with reasonable hours and good pay, as much as is paid by any other corporation of a similar character. Men who do not will never be allowed on the road again under any circumstances.

"We have never objected to labor organizations and do not now. Every man shall be free to belong to one or not, as he pleases. But the leaders of such orders can not and shall not dictate to‖this company as to whom it shall employ or how operate its property. Places that are left in obedience to the orders of the Knights of Labor shall be filled by new men, and such new men will be retained, and under no circumstances be discharged to make room for men who have left their places.

"Hereafter we shall operate this property with employees who consider their first duty is to the company and expect to obey reasonable orders made in the transaction of its business.

"There has never been a moment when, under any circumstances, we would arbitrate any‖question growing out of this strike. There has been nothing to arbitrate. It is only a question as to whether the company shall be permitted to operate its own property—a property in which there is invested over $200,000,000—or whether that property shall be controlled by the Knights of Labor.

"It may as well be understood now, and from this time on, that any wheel that is turned on the Reading system will be turned under the orders of the management of the company, and under the orders of nobody else."   (394.)

A. A. McLeod,

General Manager.

PHILADELPHIA, February 16, 1888.

AUSTIN CORBIN, Esq.,

President Philadelphia & Reading Railroad Company.

Sir: Being desirous to bring the strike in the mining region of the Reading Coal and Iron Company to a close, in order to get the working people in and about those mines to work, and speaking for those workingmen, I propose to order a resumption of work at once, upon your assurance that I can promise the men that, after they have gone to work and the mining operations are in regular progress, the subject of wages will be considered in con-ference between the company and its employees, or their representatives, and upon the further assurance that no one" shall be discriminated against by reason of his connection with the strike.   Yours, etc.,   (113.)

(Signed)   WILLIAM T. LEWIS.

PHILADELPHIA, February 17, 1888.

MR. WILLIAM T. LEWIS.

My Dear Sir: I am in receipt of your favor of this date; have consulted Mr. Keim, President of the Coal and Iron Company, in relation to its contents, and am authorized by him to say that it is substantially in accord with our position, and such action would be satisfactory to us. No one will be discriminated against because of his connection with the strike, so that it is not understood as protecting such men as have made or attempted to make personal assaults upon the men remaining at work; and provided further, that in any conference over wages, the miners are not to expect us to pay a higher rate of wages for mining than those paid by the other coal-producing companies in competition with us, namely: the Delaware, Lackawanna & Western, the Delaware & Hudson, the Lehigh Valley, the Lehigh Coal & Navigation Company, and the Lehigh & Wilkesbarre Company, but with the understanding that we are willing to adopt a basis that shall give our miners as much as is paid by either of these companies.

It is understood that the wages to be paid on returning to work will be on the old ǁ $2.50 basis, and will remain on that basis until a change shall be mutually agreed upon.

Yours truly, (219.)

AUSTIN CORBIN.

MESSRS. ALFRED SULLY AND EDWARD LAUTERBACH.

Gentlemen: I have your favor of to-day's date, and am willing to adjust all differences upon the basis therein proposed. I think the junior securities and shareholders of the company should be greatly indebted to you, and are to be congratulated upon the success of your negotiations, which will not only protect their great property from the danger of foreclosure, but preserve their proper status in the corporation. I had no other object in taking the presidency last January than to secure these results, and only consented to hold the position until reorganization was accomplished. I can not doubt that with the adoption by the syndicate of the new plan of reorganization the work is practically done, and, therefore, in order to carry out my pledge, and as an effectual answer to the charge that my desire to retain the presidency prevented an agreement upon the form of the plan of reorganization, I herewith inclose you my formal resignation as President of the Company, to be presented and take effect upon the acceptance by the reorganization trustees of the alterations and changes contained in your letter. I need scarcely add that I shall gladly aid the reorganization trustees in every way in carrying into effect their efforts to place the Reading Company on a sound financial basis. I trust most earnestly that Mr. Corbin may be induced to become my successor in the presidency, as, apart from his acknowledged ability, my personal relations with him are such as will make it a pleasure to me to give him a very loyal support. (263.)

F. B. GOWAN.

LESSON XI.

LAW AND POLITICAL CORRESPONDENCE.

OFFICE OF THE ATTORNEY-GENERAL,
BALTIMORE, April 2, 1890.

To THE GOVERNOR.

Dear Sir: I have received the letter of the Secretary of State of the 1st inst., conveying copy of the resignation of the State Treasurer, and asking, at your request, for my opinion as to whether you should "accept it or simply hold it for the present."

While the acceptance of the resignation will not, in my judgment, affect the relations of the Treasurer to the state, nor impair the obligation of his sureties, yet, as the Legislative Committee is invested with the duty of ascertaining the condition of the state bonds in his keeping, and instructed, upon proper proof, ‖to make charges against him of malfeasance or misappropriation of the bonds, as the case may be, in order that the constitutional mode of vacating the office under such circumstances shall be exercised, I do not think that you would be justified in accepting a resignation pending such inquiry now in progress by that committee.

I recommend, therefore, that the resignation be held without acceptance on your part.

Very respectfully, your obedient servant, (173.)
WM. PINKNEY WHITE,
Attorney-General.

(4)

STATE OF MARYLAND, TREASURER'S OFFICE,
March 10, 1890.

B. F. NEWCOMER,
    President Safe Deposit and Trust Company,
        Baltimore, Md.

Dear Sir: The Finance Committee of the Senate, and the Ways and Means Committee of the House, are now proceeding, under the law, to examine the assets of the state in this office, and to cancel and destroy such bonds as have been redeemed. When this is completed, the Governor and Comptroller, as members of the Board of Public Works, will complete the examination by going over the state securities in your vaults. In order that the examination may be complete, I have suggested to the Governor and Comptroller that the boxes in your building standing in my name as||Treasurer be not opened without the presence of at least one of the Board of Public Works besides myself, until all of the securities therein are counted. Their approval of this suggestion is expressed by their signatures hereto attached.   (139.)

                   STEVENSON ARCHER.

IN THE CRIMINAL COURT OF BALTIMORE.
BENCH WARRANT.
STATE OF MARYLAND VS. STEVENSON ARCHER.

To J. EDWIN WEBSTER, Esq.,
    State's Attorney for Harford County.

Sir: Application having been made to us as to the amount of bail which would be suggested to the Court by the state's officers for the appearance of the said Stevenson Archer, the accused, to answer the charge of embezzlement, as set forth in the bench warrant in the above case issued, we have consulted with the Hon. W. A. Stewart, the judge presiding in the Criminal Court of Baltimore, and, considering that a bond of $200,000 is already held by the state for the safety of the amount alleged to have been taken by the accused, and that excessive bail is not permissible under the Bill of Rights, we have concluded to advise you that in case of the issue of a *habeas corpus* by one of the judges of the Third Circuit for the Circuit Court of Harford County, bail in the sum of $25,000 be demanded by the state, with such sureties as the Circuit Court or judge thereof may approve.   (166.)

WM. PINKNEY WHYTE,
Attorney-General.

CHARLES G. KERR,
State's Attorney for Baltimore City.

Baltimore, April 12, 1890.

In my message to the General Assembly at the beginning of the session of 1890, I frankly said that I thought a new valuation and assessment of property in this state ought to be provided for.

. I remain of that opinion. I thought then that such new assessment ought to and could be made in a manner which would yield profitable results without resting on the assessing officers extraordinary and offensive powers, and without subjecting the citizen to unnecessary interference in his pivate affairs. I was then and am now of the opinion that no system of taxation ought to be made offensive to those upon whom it is intended to operate, and that no novel and extraordinary inquisitorial powers ought to be rested in subordinate taxing officers of the state. Our people are not accustomed to see such powers exercised. The bill under consideration is not framed in such a manner as to avoid these difficulties. It grants more power to the assessing officers than they ought to have, and it exposes the citizen to the malice of informers in cases where probably there would be no just cause of complaint. The effect of the bill would be, in‖my judgment, to drive more taxable property from the state than it would add to our basis of taxation. While our aim should be to encourage by all fair and just means the bringing of capital to our state, I can not, therefore, consent to be the cause of the individual, public and general discontent which would certainly follow if I approved this bill and set its machinery in motion. There are particular inconsistencies and defects in the bill upon which I might dwell at length, but it is not necessary; but I am obliged to say, although I began‖the study of the bill with a strong desire to sign it, its provisions and methods are so objectionable to me that I have finally determined it is my duty not to approve it. (334.)

I beg to call your attention to a series of libelous articles upon the late Alexander T. Stewart, and upon myself, which appeared in the New York *World* from the 14th to the 19th inst.

The articles, as will appear on the most casual inspection, are grossly libelous on their face, though they consist chiefly in groundless insinuations, assumptions and conclusio:is, and are conspicuously barren of allegations of facts. I have lived too long, and had too much experience of life, and been too much accustomed to have misrepresentation and abuse, to be disturbed by the utterances of such mendacious miscreants, and can not be compelled to buy my peace from abuse by them either by payment of money or by advertising in such an infamous sheet; nor would I think of dignifying them by bringing a civil suit for libel.

Besides, however much such libelous articles may gratify the tastes of the envious and the vicious, I know that they do not generally influence the opinions of decent men, except to inspire a disgust for the writer and publisher of them. The base motive of these articles is quite apparent to any one who knows anything of the so-called "journalism" practiced by this paper.

Had these articles been confined to libeling me I should have treated them with contemptuous silence, but when they malign the memory of my dear friend and benefactor, whose name was a synonym for high character, perfect integrity and unquestioned personal purity, as well as matchless sagacity and business success—when he is held up as the author of "a dark and secret crime;" and I know that such infamous libels are not only·false, but absolutely without the slightest foundation; in fact, I owe it to his memory that such shameless and wanton traducers should be brought to answer for their infamous crime at the bar of public justice.

It is with that purpose in view that I write this letter and send these papers, that you may exhibit these libels to the grand jury for such action as they my deem proper. (349.)

LESSON XII.

GREEN, McDONALD & COMPANY.

Gentlemen: Replying to your favor of the 10th inst., requesting reports on the financial and credit standing of Keystone Manufacturing Company, Milton W. Potter and Sage Brothers, we herewith hand you the reports asked for, and have charged you with the same.

Yours respectfully, (44.)

WILLIAM & REED,

Attorneys.

KEYSTONE MANUFACTURING COMPANY,

317 WASHINGTON STREET,

BUFFALO, ERIE COUNTY, N. Y.

May 15, 1890.

This is a corporate organization, framed March 25, 1890, under New York State laws, Act of 1848, Chapter XL, with an authorized capital of $25,000; composed of 250 shares at $100 per share; object is the manufacture of interior woodwork, artistic designs and screens; term of existence 25 years, with headquarters in Buffalo, N. Y. The officers for the first year are John D. Whitcomb,

President; Samuel D. Rose, Vice-President; John J. Goodwin, Secretary and Treasurer; and Henry Stewart, General Manager; these, with Walter Williams, form the Board of Directors for the first year.‖

Mr. Whitcomb informs us that the capital stock has been paid up in full: $15,000 in cash, which has been put into the plant and stock, and $10,000 has been paid in by virtue of patents held by Henry Stewart, who is the practical man in the business, and who has complete control of the shop and working force; that he (Whitcomb) owns $6,000 of the capital stock, and the other three (Rose, Goodwin and Williams) hold $3,000 each.

They have a good plant, well located and easily accessible to the center of trade. Goodwin and Stewart‖ give their entire personal attention to the business, and for the short time they have been in operation, have met with remarkable success, and have large orders ahead of them, notwithstanding the fact that they are working over forty hands on full time. The nature of the fine woodworking business is such as necessitate but little credit, as compared with the amount of work they turn out, for when completed, the work represents about one-seventh material and six-sevenths labor.

The patent rights can not be counted on as debt-paying assets, but there is no question but‖that they have the $15,000 at the risk of the business, and are entitled to credit thereon. They are all men of strict integrity, and are not at all likely to enter into any engagements that they would be unable to carry through, and the company is worthy of confidence. (351.)

MILTON W. POTTER,

HARDWARE AND STOVES,

316 Main St., Buffalo, Erie Co., N. Y.

Has been in the business for about fifteen years. Is doing a good business and controls a first-class line of trade. Owns his residence on Linwood Avenue, worth safely $35,000, and clear of encumbrance. The title is held jointly with his wife, to go to the survivor at death of either; owns besides this in his own name, several pieces of good real estate, clear, or nearly so, of encumbrance; carries a large stock in his store, and is worth safely $100,000 or upwards, and perfectly reliable and responsible for anything he goes into. (97.)

SAGE BROTHERS,

GROCERS,

741 Niagara St., Buffalo, Erie Co., N. Y.

Firm is composed of Thomas F. and William W. Sage. Have been in business about one year, succeeding Kinch Brothers at that time. Thomas F. Sage is a man of good character and habits, unmarried, but represents no financial responsibility; is a hard worker and attentive. William owns a house and lot on Grant Street, worth $3,500 and mortgaged for $2,500, leaving him an equity in the property of about $1,000. Business investment is small and will not exceed $1,200. They are rather slow pay at times, and in some quarters conservative houses decline to handle them except for cash. Their credit can only be quoted " fair," and cash transactions are recommended to strangers and others not already interested. (123.)

Dear Sir: I am in receipt of yours of yesterday, in answer to mine of the 3d instant, inclosing answer in the Quixote case. I must say that the action of the Court in this matter surprises me not a little. I had forgotten that the 29th ultimo was rule day, and my being in default was owing to this alone. I think the judge should allow the answer to remain on file. There are no suspicious circumstances connected with the default, the plaintiff's interests are not prejudiced, but if his Courtship is not satisfied with an oral statement from you, please advise me immediately, and I will make affidavit, stating the facts, and, I think, showing a valid defense to the action. I realize that the matter rests largely in the discretion of the Trial Court; but as this is a case of innocent forgetfulness on our part, I think it would be an abuse of this discretion for the Court to refuse to set aside the default. (169.)

Dear Sir: I am in receipt of your favor of the 2d instant, asking for my opinion on the following query: "A purchases a ticket entitling him to a reserved seat at a theatrical performance. He enters the theater, and, at the conclusion of the first act, leaves the house, and not being disposed to return, sells the pass or check received from the doorkeeper on leaving, together with the ticket for his seat, to B. Is B entitled to admission upon the pass?"

I reply as follows: The contract between the manager of the theater and the ticket-holder is a contract for the use of a certain seat by some person, *i. e.*, the holder of the ticket. It is not a contract that a certain seat shall be occupied by a certain person.   It is a contract for so much space, which the ticket-holder may occupy by himself or by his friend, or which he may leave unoccupied.   The right to use or occupy that seat or that space is, for the time being, his property; he has bought it, and he may either exercise that right himself, or he may sell or assign it to another, provided there are no personal objections to the other person.   If B is a person to whom there would have been no objections, had he been the original holder of the ticket, he is entitled to admission upon the pass.

In this connection I would call your attention to an article, "The Law of the Theater," by W. H. Whittaker, XII Law Journal, p. 390   It does not treat of the question you propound particularly, but of the law in general. (299.)

LESSON XIII.

Sir: I commiserate with you at the result of your case. You have not suffered defeat, but injustice. The only question involved has been solemnly and necessarily settled by the decision of a competent court, and the facts in your case did not warrant a departure. The ruling in your case is contrary to the policy of the courts as embodied in the maxim, *Stare decisis et non quieta movere.* Bad precedents ought not to be followed, but when a point has been settled by a competent court, when it has been deliberately adopted and declared, it ought not to be disturbed by the same court, except for very cogent reasons, and upon a clear manifestation of error. Such decisions leave us in a perplexing uncertainty as to the law. As Chancellor Kent observes: "If a decision has been made upon solemn argument and mature deliberation, the presumption is in favor of its correctness; and the community have a right to regard it as a just declaration or exposition of the law, and to regulate their actions and contracts by it."

I should be pleased to know what you contemplate now. It is unfortunate that citizens must rest in a continual state of uncertainty as to their rights and duties. The principle of precedent is eminently philosophical, and to disregard it is a very serious evil. (226.)

THE HUDSON COUNTY NATIONAL BANK,
            JERSEY CITY, N.J., August 27, 1888.
JOHN S. BELL,
        Chief Secret Service Division, Treasury.

My Dear Mr. Bell: I read in the New York *Times*'
yesterday a criticism of your testimony before the Committee of Congress investigating the engraving of cur-
rency.   I have been for twenty-five or thirty years in
banking life, and much of that time engaged in handling
bills as a teller, and it struck me that your testimony, and
that of Mr. Brooks, was pertinent and correct and in
accord with the general opinion among banks, as to the
inferior value of the present issue of silver certificates in
the matter of engraving and paper.   These notes are
issued to circulate among the general public, who are not
experts, and should be so designed as to make an imitation
of them obvious even to the uninitiated, and their true
value as a medium is in proportion to the difficulty of
successfully passing their counterfeits upon the public.

These plates seem to be designed for heavy and showy
effects, such as are customary in modern lithography, rather
than the delicate hand steel-work of former issues.   In the
latter, the least imperfection in a counterfeit destroyed the
symmetry and harmony of the note, and attracted attention
at once.   In this issue the eye is caught and retained by the
bold and striking points, and imperfections escape observation.   Consequently a fair imitation has a good chance of
passing with those not expert.   The paper seems to be too
soft and thick and does not wear well, and the engraving
seems to break down upon it much earlier than in former
issues.

Both the paper and engraving of this issue were condemned by many banking experts when they were first issued as not suited to the purpose, and I think your opinions, and those of Mr. Brooks, as expressed to the committee, will be generally||indorsed by banks and those who understand what is necessary to protect the public and whose years of experience have shown them the best means of doing so. I thought it might interest you to know this, otherwise I should not have intruded upon your valuable time. Very truly yours, (350.)

E. A. GRAHAM.

_____

THE AMERICAN EXCHANGE NATIONAL BANK,
128 BROADWAY, NEW YORK, October 4, 1888.
E. O. GRAVES,
Chief of Bureau, Washington, D. C.
Dear Sir: In reply to your note of yesterday, asking my opinion of the design, engraving and printing of the United States silver certificates of series 1886, especially of the backs, I take pleasure in saying that they seem to me to be of excellent quality in every respect. The backs of them all, which I have carefully examined, are in printing and in every particular in the best style of the engraver's art, and I see nothing in them to condemn, but everything to commend their workmanship.

I have also seen a counterfeit of each of the $1||and $5 notes. They are such miserable imitations of the genuine that a glance at them by the least experienced observer would show them to be spurious. They have never caused us annoyance. The faces of them are bad and the backs are worse. Yours very respectfully, (147.)

GEORGE S. COE,
President.

TREASURY OF THE UNITED STATES,
WASHINGTON, January 30, 1888.

HON. FRANK HISCOCK,

Chairman Sub-Committee on Finance, U. S. Senate.

Sir: I have the honor to acknowledge the receipt of your letter of the 26th instant, asking for my views as to the character of the steam-press plate-printing, its durability, and the ease with which counterfeiting may be practiced, as compared with hand-press work.

I am informed that the backs of the silver certificates of series of 1886, of the denominations of $1, $2, $5 and $10, and the backs of United States notes of the denominations of $10 and $20, have for some time been printed on presses operated by steam power, and that the backs of all other notes and certificates are printed on presses operated by hand.

The character of the printing on both the backs and faces of all the notes and certificates received from the Bureau of Engraving and Printing is perfectly satisfactory to this office, and, so far as I am informed, to the banking community and the general public. No difference in quality is observable between the backs said to be printed by hand and those said to be printed by steam. All of them appear to be of excellent quality, the color being good and the printing sharp and distinct. No complaint as to the quality of the printing has been received, though there was at first some complaint of the freshness of the printing on the new silver certificates. This arose from the necessity of issuing the certificates as soon as they were received from the Bureau of Engraving and Printing, without giving the paper and ink sufficient time to dry·

In the opinion of this office, notes should not be issued until at least six months after they are printed. As a consequence of thus holding them in a dry vault, the ink becomes thoroughly dried and hardened and the paper becomes more soft and pliable. For several months past the increase in the supply has enabled me to hold the notes and certificates for a considerable time before issuing them, and since this practice began there has been no complaint that they are not in good condition to issue.

The counterfeits of the $1 and $5 certificates, as far as they have come under the observation of this office, are much inferior to many which have appeared on previous issues of notes, and the few of them which have been received have been readily detected. I am unable to discover anything in the engraving or printing of the genuine certificates which makes it easy to counterfeit them. The work seems, on the contrary, well suited to prevent counterfeiting.

Under instructions from the Secretary of the Treasury the printing of the seals on the notes and certificates was transferred to this office from the Bureau of Engraving and Printing in July, 1885. The object of this change was to throw greater security around the printing of these certificates by rendering it impossible for that Bureau to finish them. The printing of the seals is now done in a satisfactory manner by this office from steel dies on Hoe power-presses.

It is understood that the pending bill requires these seals to be printed from steel plates on hand-roller presses. This office has not the room, the facilities, nor the experience needed to undertake this class of work. It would, therefore, be necessary to transfer the work back to the Bureau of Engraving and Printing, and to give up the security afforded by the present system, and also to greatly increase the cost of doing the work.

I deem it proper to call attention to the fact that there are now outstanding about $27,000,000 in $1 certificates and about $19,000,000 in $2 certificates, many of which have been in circulation more than two years. There being no appropriation for the payment of express charges on mutilated certificates forwarded for redemption, or on new certificates sent out to replace them, the certificates remain in circulation until badly worn, defaced, or mutliated before being presented for redemption. Many of the certificates in the hands of the people are in a condition unfit for further use, but there are no means by which the department can call them in. This condition, in my opinion, is caused by natural wear, and is not due to the method of printing the backs.

There is nothing to indicate that the certificates, the backs of which are printed by steam, are less durable than the notes and certificates, the backs of which are printed by hand.

Of $31,900,000 in $1 certificates issued to the 26th instant, less than $5,000,000 have been presented for redemption, and of the $21,000,000 in $2 certificates issued to the same date only $2,546,000 have been returned.

Respectfully yours,

JAMES W. HYATT,
Treasurer United States.

LESSON XIV.

HORACE GREELEY ON BUSINESS EDUCATION.

And so the world waits—not in one sphere, not in one place alone, but in the old countries and the new, inviting crowded hives of population to people solitary regions— waits for business men, men of capacity, men of power, men of creative thought, who know how to redeem its waste places and to render idle populations industrious and thrifty. And here it is, in my judgment, that Business Colleges will find their greatest sphere of utility; that is, not in special training for special pursuits, as too many believe to-day, but in developing a larger capacity to apprehend‖and to seize the opportunities that so abundantly exist on every side for giving new activity and new power to the creation of material wealth. The objection has been made to our old-fashioned colleges, that they are not practical. I do not think that is an accurate statement of the objection. What I would say is, that they are practical with reference to two or three pursuits, but that the demands of the time requires nine-tenths of our young men in other pursuits than those, and they are not practical in reference to these.

I know that there are to-day‖one thousand college graduates—some of them having graduated with honor at German universities—who are walking the stony streets of New York and know not how to earn a living. That is a condemnation of our university system. As a prepa-

(5)

ration for professional life—I should rather say for certain pursuits in life—it may be very well, but when I see, as I do see, so many men, whose education has cost so much, find themselves totally unable with all that to earn a living —not immoral men, not drinking men, but men, simply, who can not find‖places adapted to their capacities—when I see this I am moved to protest against a system of education which seems to me so narrow and so partial. (32S.)

ECONOMY OF TIME AND SELF-IMPROVEMENT.

There may be economy of time as well as in spending money. Time, in fact, is money, or money's worth. Few reflect deeply on this truth. Young persons in particular throw away a vast deal of time in a way often worse than useless. Much they spend in silly gossip with acquaintances, much in frivolous amusement, much in perfect vacancy of thought. In many country towns a great amount of time is spent in lounging at doorways or in the street. If all this idle time, exclusive of what should be properly devoted to open-air exercise, were spent in‖the acquisition of some kind of useful knowledge, what a difference there would be in the lot of some young people.

We say to the young, devote your leisure hours to some useful purpose. And what are your lesiure hours? Spare hours in the winter evenings after the labors of the day are over, and also hours in the morning, particularly during summer. Rising at an early hour—for instance, at 5 or 6 o'clock—may be made the means of self-culture to a very considerable extent. Science or history may be studied; languages may be learned. It is indisputable that few ever lived to a great age, and fewer still ever became distinguished, who were not in the habit of early rising. You rise late, and of course get about your business at a late hour, and everything goes wrong all day. Franklin says that, "He who rises late must trot all day, and not overtake his business at night." Dean Swift avers that "he never knew a man to come to greatness and eminence who lay in bed of a morning." We believe that, with other degenerations of our days, history will prove that late rising is a very prominent one. There seems now to be a tendency to turn day into night, to breakfast late, dine late, and go to bed late, and consequently to rise late. All this is most pernicious, both to health and morals. To a certain extent people must do as others do; nevertheless, every one is more or less able to act with something like independence of principle; the young—those who have everything to learn—can at least act upon a plan, rising at an early hour.

In order to arise early we would recommend an early hour for retiring. There are many other reasons for this; neither your eyes nor your health are so likely to be destroyed. Nature seems to have so fitted things that we ought to rest in the early part of the night. A professor used to tell his pupils that, "One hour of sleep before midnight is worth more than two after that time." Let it be a rule with you, and if possible adhered to, that you be at home and have your light extinguished by 10 o'clock in the evening. You may then rise at 6 and have eight hours sleep, which is about what nature requires. It may be most confidently affirmed that he who from his youth is in the habit of rising early will be much more likely to live to old age, more likely to be a distinguished and useful man, and more likely to pass a life that is peaceful and pleasant. Read the life of Franklin and see what he accomplished, both as respects economizing of time and the cultivation of his own capacious mind. In connection with self-improvement let us say a word on the||duty of professional diligence. It is a fact that you can not be too well made aware of that a man may distinguish himself, or at least attain great respectability in any position which is really honorable and socially useful. ✓ Whatever you do, learn to do it well. Do not be discouraged by difficulties nor vex yourselves with what may be the final results of your efforts. Just go on quietly and diligently, which will form your character and stick to you through life. The likelihood is that by this simple but persevering course—a course unmarked by any great effort—you will pass the idle and the dissipated, realizing those rewards|| which usually wait on well-directed enterprise. (707.)

LESSON XV.

PUNCTUALITY AND ITS IMPORTANCE.

The first thing I shall speak of is punctuality. I am convinced that strict punctuality ought to be classed among the positive virtues. It is based on conscience. The failure to keep an engagement by mere negligence or carelessness, or indifference, is a positive violation of the principles of honesty. It amounts to stealing some other man's time. This is true in business affairs, and it amounts to about the same thing in school and college work.

By lack of punctuality on the part of one, some other person is annoyed or hindered, or||loses time. Punctuality is a *habit*—a habit based on *principle*. Want of punctuality is also a habit, based on a practical disregard of principle.

Punctuality shows a distinct regard for the rights of other people. The root of non-punctuality is *selfishness* —some kind of selfishness. It is indolence; a disposition to let one's own comfort and ease take precedence of another's rights; or it is some piece of work one thinks will be more profitable to himself; or it is some amusement or diversion—self-indulgence at another's expense.

Sometimes the want of punctuality is the result of habitual||miscalculation. The person lays out as much or more work than can be accomplished up to a certain time, leaving no margin for going and coming, or for unforeseen contingencies. But after a man has had some fifteen hundred experiences of this sort, it would seem that he ought to learn better. There is really no excuse, and it indicates a weakness of character.

I have heard Dr. J. Adams Allen relate the following circumstance in the life of the late Dr. Gunn, the eminent surgeon: In the early days of improvement in the State of Michigan, they were residents of the same town, and co-laborers in a young medical college. One evening there was to be a faculty meeting at 7 o'clock. Dr. Gunn had been called in the morning, some twenty-five or thirty miles, to set a broken limb. He had gone across country, over the worst of roads, with a horse and gig. As the hour approached for the meeting one after another dropped in, and each one said, "Gunn won't be here, he can't make it." But said Dr. Allen, "*I told 'em he'd be there*," and sure enough at the time appointed the gig rolled up, horse and rider plastered with mud, but "Gunn was there."

I had the pleasure of listening to a course of lectures from Dr. Gunn, and I believe he never failed the class at the appointed hour but once, and then he had his place supplied. The rule was, that on the minute the door opened, "*Gunn was there.*"

When the statue of Franklin was to be unveiled in Printing House Square, New York, the hour fixed for the ceremony was 12 o'clock. All those expected to officiate were there in advance, except the clergyman. Fears were expressed that he would fail to appear. But Horace Greeley said, "You needn't be afraid; I know the man, and if he isn't dead, or some member of his family isn't dead, he'll be here." Just on the stroke of 12 the doctor entered, saying he had been delayed by a blockade in the street.

Very few young men seem to understand the value of punctuality. It is a quality a business man appreciates more and more every year of his life.

If this has not been the matter of special thought with some of you, there is no *better* time or place‖to begin than now and here. The close application of this rule of conduct for a period of six months will go far towards establishing it for a life-time; and the future will prove this to have been one of your most valuable acquisitions.

I once knew a student who was so anxious to get all he could out of a course of lectures, so fearful lest some valuable idea might escape him, that he never missed a lecture or part of a lecture, except by serious illness; and he took care to live on the same side of the‖river with the college, so he never was "*bridged*," and the professor was never so dull, or the matter of his lecture so dry, that he did not get something that paid him for being there.

Each lecture in a course is a link in a chain—the loss of one is a loss to the whole. The student frequently fails to comprehend what he hears to-day because of what he missed yesterday, and so he will be again placed at a disadvantage to-morrow.

Now you will be pleased to observed that this exhortation to promptitude is a two-edged sword;‖it cuts *this* way as well as *that*. It is an annoyance, it is a loss and an injustice to the class, for the professor to be habitually tardy and uncertain. On the other hand, it is an annoyance and an injustice, not only to the teacher, but to the whole class, for the student to be tardy and intrusive. Whenever he comes in late he treads a whole paragraph of a lecture out of sight, or makes a dash in the middle, which might be appropriately called a dash of cold water. (893.)

LINCOLN'S FAVORITE POEM.

Oh ! why should the spirit of mortal be proud ?
Like a swift flitting meteor, a fast flying cloud,
A flash of the lightning, a break of the wave,
Man passes from life to his rest in the grave.

The leaves of the oak and the willow shall fade,
Be scatter'd around and together be laid;
And the young and the old, and the low and the high
Shall molder to dust and together shall die.

The child that the mother attended and loved,
The mother that infant's affection who proved,
The husband that mother and infant who blessed,
Each,‖all, are away to their dwelling of rest.

The maid on whose cheek, on whose brow, in whose eye,
Shone beauty and pleasure, her triumphs are by;
And the memory of those who have loved her and praised,
Are alike from the minds of the living erased.

The hand of the king that the scepter hath borne,
The brow of the priest that the miter hath worn,
The eye of the sage, the heart of the brave,
Are hidden and lost in the depths of the grave.

The peasant whose lot was to sow and to reap,
The herdsman who‖climb'd with his goats to the steep,
The beggar who wandered in search of his bread,
Have faded away like the grass that we tread.

The saint who enjoy'd the communion of heaven,
The sinner who dared to remain unforgiven,
The wise and the foolish, the guilty and just,
Have quietly mingled their bones in the dust.

So the multitude goes, like the flower and the weed,
That wither away to let others succeed;
So the multitude comes, even those we behold,
To repeat every tale that hath often been told.

For we are the same our fathers have been;‖
We see the same sights that our fathers have seen,
We drink the same stream, and we feel the same sun,
And run the same course that our fathers have run.

The thoughts we are thinking our fathers would think;
From the death we are shrinking from, they too would
     shrink,
To the life we are clinging to, they too would cling;
But it speeds from the earth like a bird on the wing.

They loved, but their story we can not unfold;
They scorn'd, but the heart of the haughty is cold;
They grieved, but no wail from their‖slumber will come;
They joy'd, but the voice of their gladness is dumb.

They died--aye ! they died; and we things that are now,
Who walk on the turf that lies over their brow,
Who make in their dwellings a transient abode,
Meet the changes they met on their pilgrimage road.

Yea, hope and despondence, and pleasure and pain,
Are mingled together in sunshine and rain;
And the smile and the tear, the song and the dirge,
Still follow each other like surge upon surge.

'T is the wink of an eye, 't is the draught of a breath,
From the blossom‖of health to the paleness of death,
From the gilded saloon to the bier and the shroud,
Oh! why should the spirit of mortal be proud?   (526.)

LESSON XVI.

EXTRACTS FROM AN ADDRESS

By Hon. A. H. Colquitt, LL. D., Ex-Governor of
Georgia.

If you young ladies and gentlemen have never been
impressed with the serious import of life, surely this night
will make this impression upon you in undying characters.
What an impressive scene is this; what is the meaning of it?
This crowded arena, these over-hanging galleries,
these looks of interest and anxiety on this circle of
young ladies and gentlemen. What is the significance of
this vast multitude of men and women? It is this: That
these youths of both sexes to-night are starting out upon
the career of life, and here are the eyes of fond parents,
here are the eyes of warm and cordial friends, here are
the eyes of patriots and Christians, looking with deep
solicitude and anxiety into each face that is in my presence to-night; and the inquiry of every heart is: What is
to be the fortune, what is to be the destiny of this, my
friend; will it be success or disappointment, will it be
triumph or defeat, will it be joy or sorrow, will it be light
or darkness?

What this institution has done for you, though it may
be whatever human intelligence or invention could suggest, after all it is in your power to render all these advantages entirely unavailing. Parents may watch over you

and pray for 'you, teachers may labor in all good conscience for your behoof, the treasures of science may be
freely thrown open to you, the benefits of travel may be
given to you, and after all, if a proper self-respect and self-
culture is lacking your lives can be nothing better than a
splendid failure. Let it be known now and forever that
no great character comes by inheritance. Work, work ;
faith, faith! is the condition by which human intelligence
arrives at a real and honest fame.

By another's sweat you may eat bread; by another's
care and money you may be lapped in ease; by another's
hard-earned millions you may succeed to the power that
money confers, such as it is, but to hope for a royal road
to true greatness, or goodness, is folly, and you will never
find it. Then, how important it is for your future lives,
my young friends, that very early in these lives you should
begin the study of your own individuality. Men all differ
in habits, dispositions and capacities, and, in my judgment,
the true foundation upon which to build human develop-
ment is each man's own individuality. No two boys study
alike, commit to memory alike, read alike, or compose
alike. Then, let each man see what is the most convenient and best method for him to work upon,
and then, above all things, be in earnest, diligent
in business, fervent in spirit. It is to be as the
Divine Master enjoins and would have us to be.
In forming your character never be without a purpose. If the purpose could be wisely selected, there
should never be a doubt about it. The child of genius, if
he may be said to be born, is born of an undying purpose

and wish to be just what he becomes. Rest assured, my young friends, that the unstable man can never succeed. Life is too short; and, at best, our progress through darkness is too slow for our minds forever to be starting out from new points of departure, and for new objects.

Is it not a strange thing how little we do for the comfort, the pleasure, or the gratification of one another? I may be poor, and I am; it is no secret where I live. I may not be able to do anything for my fellow-creatures in the way of money, but I can do this—and though I have passed what is considered the middle period of life, if there is anything I feel thankful to God for, it is that I have retained the sensibilities that make me feel for the woes of my fellow-man. [Applause.] I may not be able to give him money for his relief, I may not be able to succor him from poverty, but, he is my fellow-man, and I may meet him on the street, and I may see the marks of care upon his brow, and his shoulders bent beneath the burden that he is carrying, I can at least take him by the hand and say, " God bless you! here is my hand and my heart to encourage you and bid you to hope." I can do this. [Applause.]

I wish to refer to one other thing, and then I shall close, because I know these college rules are very strict, and I know what used to be the penalty for breaking them. I want to present one idea to the young men as a warning. One of the beguiling evils of to-day is skepticism in special forms. And what is there in skepticism that attracts young men? The trouble is not that they will

deny the Bible, or the teachings of a godly mother and
saintly father, but there is many a young man who comes
out of college and hears people say, " That is an educated
man." He thinks it is so, and endeavors to prove it by
thinking something that nobody else thinks, and talking
and acting like nobody else talks or acts. He says, " I
will dive down into‖the earth, and will search for information, and discover the hidden truths." He would have you
know that he is one of the smartest fellows, looking away
out yonder and thinking for himself, and with that kind
of ideas the young men are propping themselves up in
false beliefs. They will give you to understand that they
are wiser, more learned, more independent in their opinions
and their thoughts than other young men of the country,
because they can deny what they can not understand. I
have seen it, I have heard it; they want the world to
believe that‖they will credit nothing that they don't know
something about. Don't tell them about God and Providence, they must see; they must know and understand by
logical deduction or sequences or they will not believe,
and yet you might put the question to one of these gentlemen, and he could not tell you, to save his life, how his
finger-nails grew. Be true to yourselves; and above all
things, as the learned Doctor said to-night, carry the love
of home with you in all the avenues of life and wherever
you may go. There is always hope‖for a young man if
he venerates father and mother—if he can look back on
the old homestead and remember ·when sister and he
swung on the old gate under the old oak. I can tell you
that the devil and his colleagues, and all the combined

hosts of this world, can not lead astray the young man who loves father and mother and the home circle. [Applause.]

Another word and I am done. It is a grand thing to be young; it is a grand thing to see youth in the flush of early manhood and womanhood, with the ‖sun high up in the heavens. It is a grand thing to see a young man that stands in the midst of the rush of the passions of his own nature, with temptations all around him, who is able to say to all assailants striving to contaminate him, "I am free and pure, and uncontaminated by these." It is a grand thing to see a young man resist all these temptations, and it is a grand thing to see an old man, upon whose head have fallen the snows of life, able to say in the last hours of manhood‖and life that is soon to be gone, "I have lived long, I have mingled in the midst of the scenes and vicissitudes of life, and yet I stand to say that I have never seen the righteous forsaken nor his seed begging bread."

I bid you God-speed, young ladies and young gentlemen, and after you have reaped all the fruits, and the honors, and the happiness that this life can bestow, I trust that if I and these older ones shall precede you to the grave, we shall be there before you to welcome you as you shall‖plant your feet upon the golden streets of the New Jerusalem, bearing golden rewards as the harvest of your lives. [Applause.] (1,421.)

LESSON XVII.

BUSINESS ADVICE.

My object is to point out to you, as briefly as possible, the way to become a "man of business," and, in doing this, all that I aim at is to give, from my own experience, such hints as will be found practically useful. "How to get money" is now the order of the day—"the one thing needful," so far as worldly matters are concerned. It is, I admit, an awkward thing to begin the world without a dollar; and yet hundreds of individuals have raised large fortunes from a single shilling. I know a gentleman, a builder, now worth two hundred thousand dollars, who was a bricklayer's laborer forty years ago, at eight shillings per day. He became rich by acting upon principle. He has frequently assured me that, even when he was in this employment, he contrived to save three shillings a day out of his earnings, and thus laid by $100 per annum. From this moment his fortune was made. Like a hound, upon the right scent, the game, sooner or later, was sure to become his own. He possessed an indomitable spirit of industry, perseverance and frugality, and the first $100 he realized became the foundation for thousands. The world at large would call this man fortunate, and ascribe his prosperity to good luck; but the world would be very wrong in doing so. If there was any luck at all in the matter, it was the luck of possessing a clear head and active hands, by means of which multitudes of others have carved out their own fortunes, as well as the person to whom I allude. Franklin and Girard may be mentioned as instances of this; they adapted the means to the end—a process which commands a never-failing success. In brief, they were men of business. By "business" I mean habit. Paradoxical as it may appear at first sight, business is nothing in the world but habit, the soul of which is regularity. Like the fly-wheel upon a steam engine, regularity keeps the motion of life steady and unbroken, thereby enabling the machine to do its work unobstructedly. Without "regularity" your notions as a man of business may be excellent, but they will never be profitable. Picture to yourself a ship without a rudder, a lock without a key, a house without a roof, or a carriage without wheels; these are types of all attempts to do business without regularity, all useless. The force of example is the greatest force in the world, because it is the force of habit—which has been truly and appropriately called a second nature. Its overwhelming influence is so great that honest men become rogues by contact. Do you imagine yourself exempt from the contagion? If strong-minded men have frequently fallen victims to evil examples, how shall the weak escape? Very easily. Do not submit yourself to it. The preliminaries of temptation are easily to be avoided, however difficult the subsequent coils may be to unwind. If you mean to make your way in the world, look about you and insure your well-doing by copying the habits and following the example of those only whose conduct, experience and success entitle them to the character of models.

The first thing you will have to attend to on commencing as a tradesman is the choice of a situation for a shop. In doing this always bear in mind the fact that "a rolling stone gathers no moss." Hundreds of tradesmen have been wrecked upon the postulate, "this will do for the present." The "present"‖is always the golden moment of your life. Clutch it with a firm grasp. Fix upon a shop in which you may stay as long, as you live. Recollect there is much truth in the assertion that "three removes are as bad as a fire." Having obtained the shop you want, do not put an article into it until you have secured a lease of it. No one should be a tenant at will. If by care and strict attention to business you make a stand more valuable than before, it will be the "will" of the landlord that you‖turn out, and, unless you are pretty certain of doing this, you have no object in taking a shop at all. Steady improvement in a retail business is invariably local. He who employs years of his time in forming and consolidating a valuable connection would be esteemed a madman to remove from the situation which gave birth to it to another where it would be lost, and yet the non-possession of a lease of the place you occupy will very frequently accomplish the same end. In a word, if your business depends upon customers, get them, and keep them by staying where you are. Do not listen to the advice which certain officious friends and foolish people are continually in the habit of offering without consideration. "Don't hamper yourself with a lease," say they, which, being interpreted into any thing intelligible, means: "Don't secure the only means of security." A lease to a tradesman is what an anchor is

(6)

to a ship—the only hold-fast to be relied on. A business once commenced and a connection once formed, can not be removed without much loss and considerable inconvenience. Having taken possession of your premises, let your first care‖be to insure them, as well as your stock in trade, against fire. This is one of the duties most incum-bent upon a young tradesman. If the house which he inhabits, as well as all the goods in his shop, were positively his own (that is to say, were actually paid for), it would be one of the most absurd things upon earth to neglect the means of providing a remedy against the overwhelming consequences of fire, more especially when such remedy is obtainable without the slightest difficulty or trouble. But in the other, and more common case, where the‖goods are not morally his own, inasmuch as his creditors have not been paid for them, the neglect of this precaution becomes absolutely criminal. If a tradesman who has been enabled to obtain goods upon credit, hesitates or neglects to insure them against fire, and they should afterwards be consumed, and he be unable to pay for them in consequence, however much others may mince the matter, the simple fact will be that he has negatively robbed those who confided in him. Neglect this precaution and I should feel no pity for you if your stock and furniture were all‖destroyed by fire! It would be nonsense to affirm that capital is not necessary in business; and yet I have known many who have risen to great affluence without it, in the first instance. Assuming that you have little or none to begin with, your task will be more difficult than if you had sufficient funds at your command. But do not let the want of money intimidate you. If you are sincere in your intentions, if you are favored with an average quantity of common sense, and withal industrious, temperate and economical, you need not let the want of capital be a stumbling block in your way. If you are respectable, straightforward, and acquainted with the business you are about to undertake, you will find no difficulty in obtaining credit sufficient to enable you to open shop to advantage. But you must recollect that in this case you will be trading upon other people's money; and it behooves you, as a consequence, to manage your business with the strictest economy and prudence. "Money makes money," is a vulgar but true adage. Argument would be supererogatory in proving the advantages which capital affords to its possessor. But there are two ways of using it—a right and a wrong. The only legitimate use of capital is to be out of debt. To be out of debt, under any circumstances, is an inestimable blessing, but more particularly so in mercantile business, where pecuniary obligations are, of necessity, much larger than in private or personal affairs. I do not envy that man, who, having one thousand dollars in capital, endeavors to trade upon twenty; and yet this is done more frequently than otherwise. Assuming his speculation to be fortunate, the means are so ill adapted to the end, that a constant oscillation of feeling and anxiety is invariably created in consequence. Keep within bounds, is the best advice that can be given to any one with a moderate capital.

LESSON XVIII.

BUSINESS ADVICE.—*Continued.*

Over-trading is the great bane of most young trades-men. Naturally anxious "to do business," they forget that buying and selling do not necessarily imply profit-able transactions, and they are too often disappointed when the debtor and creditor sides come together, to find that they have gained their trouble for their re-muneration. It is much better to do a little business safely, than a great deal which is tinged with any matter of doubt.‖ Bitter experience has taught those who seek to do an over-large business at small profits, that very little credit can be given; since the only inducement for reducing prices below an average standard is a certainty of payment. ⤲If you do business with all the world, you may rely upon having a world of trouble and anxiety in return; and, after all, the net profit upon an extensive business carried on in this way is seldom more than would be realized without a tenth part of the trouble. My advice to you is, to establish and maintain a local business.‖ As it is almost impossible to carry on such a business with-out giving credit, you must weigh well in your mind before-hand to what extent you may with propriety do so. The amount of credit you take will, of course, depend upon the amount you give. If you are doing a safe and current business, you need fear little on this head; only take care in making your purchases to bargain for time sufficient. This is important if you have a capital, but absolutely indispensable if you have none. In giving credit, there should be a caution without mistrust; and,‖ when debts are contracted with parties that become embarrassed in their circumstances, it is often of great importance for the creditor to be indulgent without negligence, and firm without rigor. When a tradesman is in the habit of giving credit to any extent, and his capital is limited, it follows, of necessity, that he must also take credit himself. Here we see the evil of the system. To preserve his own character, he must, of course, make good his payments on the very day whereon they become due; whereas, his customers only pay their debts when it suits them,‖ and very frequently not all! It is not my intention to go fully into the question of the pernicious system of credit, seeing that in some cases it must be given; but I warn all tradesmen from trusting any but those whom they know to be respectable and honorable people. A man who does business to the amount of only $500 per annum, and receives his money, is doing better than he who sells on credit $5,000 at the risk of losing one-half of the amount by bad debts. Small profits and quick returns are better than long credits and enormous profits. The one is sure game, the other doubtful. I would have you bear in mind that it is easier to increase than to dispose of your purchases; therefore be cautious not to buy more goods than you are likely to have a quick sale for. Let what you buy be of the best quality—cheap articles are dear at any price. Whatever goods your customers may order, of course you will procure for them; but you would do wrong were you to recommend them. If you have a large number of empty shelves, many‖methods may be devised for filling them without purchasing heavy and expensive stock for that purpose. From the great and unavoidable losses sustained by the "credit system," a man who has ready money can buy with immense advantage to himself, by always paying cash for his goods. If, in addition to this, he has sufficient cash in hand to defy the larger houses, and will sell "for cash only," he may realize a fortune in a few years. Once let an establishment be noted for "cheap bargains," and purchasers will flock to it as instinctively as sharks to a ship!‖ "Civility is cheap," says the old proverb. That, perhaps, is the reason why it is so cultivated. If a man would thrive in trade he must learn to be civil, and even polite, on all occasions and to all sorts of customers. A connection is not soon formed, and can only be secured by unwearied attention to business. The tradesman must study the whims and caprices of his customers in every particular; and if they occupy his time for hours, and in the end lay out no more than a shilling, still he must appear satisfied, and by no means‖out of temper. I do not err in affirming that one individual who is methodical in his business can, with ease, perform the work of six men who set order and regularity at defiance. The one, by unity of action, clears as he goes; the latter make work for each other; and, after all, nothing is done properly. A merchant or tradesman must be peremptory on this point; every day furnishes employment enough of itself, and there needs no accumulation of what ought to have been done the day previously. On commencing business, economy should be the first consideration. It‖is useless to employ more hands about your establishment than you can keep constantly at work. It is better, as a rule, to give a liberal salary to one industrious young man who has your interest at heart, than to employ several clerks at low salaries, of whom you know little or nothing. Your own time, also, should be exclusively devoted to business, which will effect a saving of at least six salaries. Acting upon this principle, whether you employ few or many assistants, you will find that your best interests are consulted. A man of business, without his‖diary, or engagement book, is like a body without a soul—incapable of action. To have a perfect and complete register of all your engagements for days and weeks to come is no indifferent matter to any one who desires to be punctual, and prepared for them, especially when the means are at hand. One of the first principles with the man of business should be not to depend upon his recollection for anything. If orders arrive, if bills are to be paid or received, if appointments are made for any purpose whatever, in fact, if anything is to be‖done, set it down in writing. To do this, however, to any advantage, it must be, like everything else, done by system; for an irregular and heterogeneous mass of memoranda can be of no use to any one. The arrangement should insure prompt information. For this purpose prepare a small book ruled with divisions for each day in the week, and arrange the days, dates, months, etc., according to the nature and extent of your engagements. In this book you should enter, in advance, every appointment that has been made, everything that has to be done, and all moneys that are‖to be paid or received on particular days. By turning to this diary every morning, regularly, the business of the day will be at once apparent, and nothing can by any possibility be forgotten or overlooked. Show me a man who keeps his appointments, and I will show you a man of business. A tradesman should never be behind his time one minute. Attention to this apparently minor consideration has been the making of thousands of individuals. It proves a man to be active and industrious, and one who is alive to all the duties of his calling. It causes‖him to be well spoken of, and creates a confidence in his integrity that may be of vast service to him through life. In my multifarious transactions with the world, I have seen so many and so great evils resulting from a want of punctuality, that I feel bound to urge its observance as a most solemn duty.

LESSON XIX.

BUSINESS ADVICE.—*Continued.*

On the coast of Norway there is a whirlpool one hundred miles in diameter, into the verge of which, if any thoughtless mariner allows his ship to venture, inevitable destruction is the result.   At first, all appears fair and pleasant sailing, the‖bark moves round without any perceptible danger; but gradually the speed increases, until, with a frightful velocity, it is hurried round the circling vortex, and, in a moment, is swallowed up by the devouring gulf.   Such a fate awaits all tradesmen who endeavor to establish a business upon artificial credit, by means of accommodation bills.   The relief which is obtained is temporary; the penalty, durable.   At first, as in the case of the vessel, all appears plain and pleasant; but a day of reckoning must come.   None but persons well versed in the details of business are acquainted with the‖destructive nature of this artificial credit.   If A accepts an accommodation bill from B, which one or the other gets discounted, as is very often the case, for mutual accommodation—that is, by dividing the proceeds between both—it follows, as a matter of course, that both are equally bound for its payment when it becomes due.   But instead of doing this, they are tempted by the first facility to try a second, and thus endeavor to avoid the actual payment of cash when the bill becomes due, by creating another and getting it discounted, in like manner, to pay ‖the first with. The effects of all this may be easily foreseen. Each of the bills thus manufactured becomes larger in amount than the one which preceded it, in order to provide for interest, etc. At last the bubble breaks. One or both of the parties fail, discount is no longer to be obtained, and bankruptcy winds up the whole. One false step of this kind is always sure to be followed by others. It is fatal to a young man's character and prospects. A tradesman who dabbles in accommodation bills is not safe to be trusted at all! A volume ‖ might be written on the fatal consequences which result from speculation, in the course of only a single year. A young man, with a small capital, takes a shop and stocks it with what he considers necessary. Fancying, however, that he does not do nearly so much business as his neighbors, and being unwilling to get rich in the good old-fashioned way, and to rise by degrees, he sets his wits to work to find out the reason. This he soon ascertains to be, as he imagines, the inferiority of the goods he has selected, and the insignificant ‖ "show" he has made. Finding his credit good, he forthwith proceeds to order the most expensive articles, and, determined to eclipse his brother tradesmen, he sets them forth to the best advantage. ⟨ Henceforth he becomes reckless. Having no longer money of his own, he is aware that he must raise sufficient to pay his bills as they become due, and therefore other tradesmen must suffer, and fresh goods be added to his already extensive stock. This can not last forever; sacrifices are made to meet present exigencies, and eventually a failure takes place, an assignment is made, under which, perhaps, a‖dividend is declared of ten cents on the dollar! ⌐The young man in business, in a case of distress, can obtain from a stranger infinitely greater commiseration, and always more relief, than he can from his friends or relatives; for "pity is poor relief." An application for a trifling loan is met by one's friends with a thousand hem's and ha's! First comes a lecture on imprudence, next the necessity of caution, then a hint that you are a novice in your business, and that if they lent you the sum you would be none the better for it, etc.‖ If your relatives condescend to deal with you, there are continual complaints of the commodities with which they are supplied. They fancy you buy your goods cheap, for the purpose of making them pay dearly for them. In short, there is no giving satisfaction; therefore, my young friends, if you are willing to take my advice, you will live totally independent, in money matters, of all your kindred. If you succeed in the world, and are well off, then, indeed, they will flock around your standard, and say everything that is good of you, because you are not likely‖to borrow money.

The time has been when a verbal contract between two parties would be considered binding. The world since then has changed; and in order to be perfectly safe from loss or injury I advise my readers to deal with every man and woman as if they were rogues. As for friends, still greater precautions are needful with them. Let nothing of any moment whatever be undertaken without its being first penned down in black and white, and signed in the presence of a witness. You have then some data to go upon, and can right yourself in case of necessity in a court of law. A want of attention to these points in early life cost me some thousands of dollars. I paid dearly for my experience, but if I may yet be serviceable to my fellow-tradesmen, the money will not have been altogether thrown away. A man who has any feeling of honor about him would rather die outright than become a bankrupt, and any sacrifice that he could make he would willingly consent to. Misfortune is one thing, imprudence is another, and knavery the climax. When a man is unfortunate, he is deservedly an object of sympathy. To such I would say, the moment you find yourself in difficulties, and perceive that you can not honestly extricate yourself without speculating with what does not belong to you, call a private meeting of your creditors, and lay before them the entire state of your affairs. Make a proposition of what you think you will be able to pay towards the liquidation of their claims, and trust to their generosity to accept it. You will then be taken by the hand by all your creditors, get a release, and perhaps, with their kind assistance, become a better man than you were. But keep nothing back. Having briefly enumerated the instructions I had in view, I come now to the end of my task. Some will say, "There is no need of advice to a man who has made a fortune, and is about to retire from business." I beg pardon, and hope such will take warning by the following: Not long since an active young man of my acquaintance had, by good luck and unwearied attention to business, and a perfect knowledge of it in all its branches, laid by sufficient to enable him to retire from active‖pursuits of life. He mentioned his views to a friend of his, who eagerly heard him out, and joyfully accepted his proposals, which were to take his business, furniture, stock in trade, etc.; and to oblige his friend who made the purchase, he consented, after some entreaties, to take his notes for the amount (several thousand dollars). He took them—they were never paid. His friend, it turned out, had no money, but contrived to keep the game alive for a few months, by speculating like a madman, and then suffered shipwreck, defrauding his creditors to an immense amount.‖ (4,000.)

LESSON XX.

ELEMENTS OF SUCCESS.

ADDRESS BY JAMES A. GARFIELD BEFORE AN ASSEMBLY OF STUDENTS.

Ladies and Gentlemen: I have consented to address you this evening chiefly for two reasons: one of them personal to myself, the other public. The personal reason is that I have a deep and peculiar sympathy with young people who are engaged in any department of education. Their pursuits are to me not only matters of deep interest, but of profound mystery. It will not, perhaps, flatter you older people when I say that I have far less interest in you than in these young people. With us the great questions of life are measurably settled. Our days go on,∥their shadows lengthen as we approach nearer to that evening which will soon deepen into the night of life; but before these young people are the dawn, the sunrise, the coming noon—all the wonders and mysteries of life. For ourselves, much of all that belongs to the possibilities of life is ended, and the very angels look down upon us with less curiosity than upon these, whose lives are just opening. Pardon me, then, if I feel more interest in them than in you.

I feel a profounder reverence for a boy than a man. I never meet a∥ragged boy of the street without feeling that I may owe him a salute, for I know not what possibilities may be buttoned up under his shabby coat. When I meet you in the full flush of mature life, I see nearly all

there is of you; but among these boys are the great men
of the future—the heroes of the next generation, the philosophers, the statesmen, the philanthropists, the great
reformers and moulders of the next age. Therefore, I
say, there is a peculiar charm to me in the exhibitions of
the young people engaged in the business of education.

But there was a reason of public policy which brought
me here to-night, and it was to testify to the importance
of these Business Colleges, and to give two or three
reasons why they have been established in the United
States. I wish every college President in the United
States could hear the first reason I propose to give. Business Colleges, my fellow-citizens, originated in this country as a protest against the insufficiency of our system of
education—as a protest against the failure, the absolute
failure, of our American schools and colleges to fit young
men and women for the business of life. Take the great
classes graduated from the leading colleges of the country
during this and the next month, and how many, or rather,
how few, of their members are fitted to go into the practical business of life and transact it like sensible men?
These Business Colleges furnish their graduates with a
better education for practical purposes than either Prince-
ton, Harvard or Yale.

The people are making a grave charge against our
system of higher education when they complain that it is
disconnected from the active business of life. It is a charge
to which our colleges can not plead guilty and live. They
must rectify the fault, or miserably fail of their great purpose. There is scarcely a more pitiable sight than to see

here and there learned men, so called, who have graduated in our own and the universities of Europe with high honors—men who know the whole gamut of classical learning—who have sounded the depths of mathematical and speculative philosophy—and yet who could not harness a horse or make out a bill of sale if the world depended upon it. [Applause.]

The fact is that our‖curriculum of college studies was not based on modern ideas, and has not grown up to our modern necessities. The prevailing system was established at a time when the learning of the world was in Latin and Greek; when, if a man would learn arithmetic, he must first learn Latin; and if he would learn the history and geography of his country, he could acquire the knowledge only through the Latin language. Of course, in those days, it was necessary to lay the foundation of learning in a knowledge of the learned languages. The universities of Europe, from which our‖colleges were copied, were founded before the modern languages were born. The leading languages of Europe are scarcely six hundred years old. The reasons for a course of study then are not good now. The old necessities have passed away. We now have strong and noble living languages, rich in literature, replete with high and earnest thought, the languages of science, religion and liberty, and yet we bid our children feed their spirits on the life of dead ages, instead of the inspiring life and vigor of our own times. I do not object to classical learning; far from it;‖but I would not have excluded the living present. Therefore I welcome the Business College in the form it has taken in the United

States, because it meets an acknowledged want by affording to young people of only common scholastic attainments, and even to the classes that graduate from Harvard and Yale, an opportunity to learn important and indispensable lessons before they go out into the business of life.

The present Chancellor of the British Exchequer, the Right Honorable Robert Lowe, one of the brightest minds in that kingdom, said in a recent address before the venerable university at Edinburgh: "I was a few months ago in Paris, and two graduates of Oxford went with me to get our dinner at a restaurant, and if the white-aproned waiter had not been better educated than all three of us, we might have starved to death. We could not ask for our dinner in his language, but, fortunately, he could ask us in our own language what we wanted." There was one test of the insufficiency of modern education. [Applause.]

LESSON XXI.

ELEMENTS OF SUCCESS.—*Continued.*

There is another reason—the last I shall give in illustrating the importance of Business Colleges—and that is the consideration which was so beautifully and cogently urged a few moments since, by a young lady who delivered the valedictory of her class, that it is almost surplusage to add a word to her discussion.   The career opened in Business Colleges for young women is a most important and noteworthy feature of these institutions.

Laugh at it as we may, put it aside as a jest if we will, keep it out of Congress or political campaigns, still, the woman question is rising in our horizon larger than the size of a man's hand, and some solution, ere long, that question must find.   I have not yet committed my mind to any formula that embraces the whole question.   I halt on the threshold of so great a problem.   But there is one point on which I have reached a conclusion, and that is, that this nation must open up new avenues of work and usefulness to the women of the country, so that everywhere they may have something to do.   This is, just now, infinitely more valuable to them than the platform or the ballot-box.   Whatever conclusion shall be reached on that subject by-and-by, at present the most valuable gift which can be bestowed on women is something to do, which they can do well and worthily, and thereby maintain themselves.

Therefore I say that every thoughtful statesman will look with satisfaction upon such Business Colleges as are opening a career for our young women. On that score we have special reason to be thankful for the establishment of these institutions. [Applause.]

Now, young gentlemen, let me for a moment address you touching your success in life, and I hope the very brevity of my remarks will increase the chance of their making a lodgment in your minds.‖ Let me beg you, in the outset of your career, to dismiss from your minds all idea of succeeding by luck. There is no more common thought among young people than that foolish one that by-and-by something will turn up by which they will suddenly achieve fame or fortune. No, young gentlemen, things don't turn up in this world unless somebody turns them up. Inertia is one of the indispensable laws of matter, and things lie flat where they are until by some intelligent spirit (for nothing but spirit makes motion in this world) they are endowed with‖activity and life. Do not dream that some good luck is going to happen to you and give you fortune. Luck is an *ignis fatuus.* You may follow it to ruin, but not to success. The great Napoleon, who believed in his destiny, followed it until he saw his star go down in blackest night, when the Old Guard perished around him, and Waterloo was lost. A pound of pluck is worth a ton of luck.

Young men talk of trusting to the spur of the occasion. That trust is vain. Occasions can not make spurs, young gentlemen. If you‖expect to wear spurs you must win them. If you wish to use them you must buckle them to your own heels before you go into the fight. Any success you may achieve is not worth the having unless you fight for it. Whatever you win in life you must conquer by your own efforts, and then it is yours—a part of yourself. [Applause.]

Again, in order to have any success in life, or any worthy success, you must resolve to carry into your work a fulness of knowledge—not merely a sufficiency, but more than a sufficiency. In‖this respect, follow the rule of the machinists. If they want a machine to do the work of six horses, they give it nine-horse power, so that they may have a reserve of three. To carry on the business of life you must have surplus power. Be fit for more than the thing you are now doing. Let every one know that you have a reserve in yourself; that you have more power than you are now using. If you are not too large for the place you occupy, you are too small for it. How full our coun-try‖is of bright examples, not only of those who occupy some proud eminence in public life, but in every place you may find men going on with steady nerve, attracting the attention of their fellow-citizens, and carving out for them-selves names and fortunes from small and humble begin-nings and in the face of formidable obstacles.

Young gentlemen, let not poverty stand as an obstacle in your way. Poverty is uncomfortable, as I can testify, but nine times out of ten the best thing that can happen to a young man is to be tossed over-board and compelled to‖ sink or swim for himself. In all my acquaintances I have never known one to be drowned who was worth the saving.

One thought more and I will close. This is almost a sermon, but I can not help it, for the occasion itself has given rise to the thoughts I am offering you. Let me suggest that in giving you being God locked up in your nature certain forces and capabilities. What will you do with them? Look at the mechanism of a clock. Take off the pendulum and ratchet and the wheels go rattling down, and all its‖force is expended in a moment ; but properly balanced and regulated it will go on, letting out its force tick by tick, measuring hours and days, and doing faithfully the service for which it was designed. I implore you to cherish and guard and use well the force that God has given to you. You may let them run down in a year, if you will. Take off the strong curb of discipline and morality and you will be an old man before your twenties are passed. Preserve these forces. Do not burn them out with brandy, or waste them‖in idleness and crime. [Applause.] Do not destroy them. Do not use them unworthily. Save and protect them that they may save for you fortune and fame. Honestly resolve to do this and you will be an honor to yourself and to your country. I thank you, young friends, for your kind attention. [Applause.] · (2,054.)

LESSON XXII.

IS THE WORLD BETTER OR WORSE?

ADDRESS BY DOCTOR TALMAGE.

Ladies and Gentlemen: If we leave it to the evolutionists to guess where we came from and to the theologians to prophesy where we are going to, it still remains to us to be satisfied that we are here. [Laughter and applause.] And we are glad to be here under such interesting circumstances to take part in the anniversay celebration of an institution famous as the exemplar of a great practical system of business education.

When I was a boy we used to have a saying that there was no royal road to learning, but there is now a royal road. We find it through the college of business. The children then used to cry because they had to go to school, now they cry if they have to stay at home.   There are means of acquiring knowledge in practical institutions like this, and multitudes of others, in all lands; and there are discoveries and advances in education such as our ancestors never dreamed of. We remember when astronomy was considered a luxury in education. Now it is as useful and practical as agriculture. Within fifty years the world has been revolutionized. The world is better.

I congratulate this college and I congratulate these young men and these young women. I have been look-

ing at them while I sat here. I can tell that they mean
honest work, and the world will open before them and
the victory will be achieved. Each one of these young
people will get a call from God to do some one thing that
no one else in the universe can do. Talk about ministers
getting a call from God to preach, all of them must, but every
person is called of God to do some one thing. God sends
no one on a fool's errand, and out of the fourteen hundred
millions of the race there is not one that can do your work.
Find out just what you are to do; it is all written in your
physical or mental or spiritual constitution; get your call
directly from the throne of God for this one thing, and
then marshall all your faculties and gather them into companies and regiments and battalions; then ride along the
line and give the word of command, "Forward, march,"
and there is no power on earth or hell that can stand
before you. [Applause.]

The world is pretty much what we make it. God
made it in the first place, but every man makes it over
again. Show me a man's spectacles and I will tell you
what kind of a world he makes. If he looks through
blue spectacles, it is a blue world; if they are green
spectacles, it is a green world; if yellow spectacles, it is a
jaundiced world; and if transparent spectacles, it is the
glorious, bright, beautiful world that God made it. The
first thing a man wants is to have his heart right, and the
next is to have his liver right. If they are right he is all
right, for he sees the world in the right way. It is said
that one of the Rothschilds was approached by a man
armed with a pistol, who demanded that the rich man

divide his millions. Rothschild explained that, as there were about as many millions of people in France as he had money, the would-be highwayman was probably entitled, on his own basis of sharing, to only one dollar, "which," he said, "I will promptly pay you," and so ended this socialistic argument.

Everything depends upon the way of putting things. The most complaints are made by men in perfect health, who have wealth and leisure and friends. In the six thousand years of the world's existence there must have been, according to my calculation, about two millions of bright days. How dare we complain? Man wants, first, competence; second, superfluity; third, affluence; fourth, MORE! [Laughter and applause]. It takes a man with all the luxuries to be thoroughly miserable. One day I was riding along and overtook a lame man laboriously making his way on crutches, and I asked him if he wanted to ride. He said he would be glad to, and I helped him up as gently as I could, and he began to tell me of the multitude of his blessings and mercies. True, he was lame and poor, and he had lost friends, but God was so good to him that he found something to thank Him for every day. He had food and shelter and clothing—all that one could wish. And when we came to where he wanted to stop, and he alighted and thanked me, and told me I had been feet to the lame, and asked God to bless me, I couldn't have told whether I had given him a ride or he had given me one. The virtue of a cheerful spirit is one of the causes of happiness. I once paid seven dollars to hear Jenny Lind sing. I would not pay a cent to hear a man groan. [Laughter.] It is not what we get, but what we are, that makes true happiness.

We see too much to find fault with. There are not so many people in the world who are bad—that is, who mean to be bad. Most of those who do wrong are the victims of circumstances. They would be better if they could, and if we had been rocked in the cradle of crime, as they were, we should probably have done as badly as they—perhaps worse. With your five hundred faults, you ought to let another man have one. [Laughter.] I am afraid the imperfections of others will kill some of us. Every man who has done some good work for God has had the hounds of criticism after him. The world is not worse than it used to be, and you never can make it better by scolding at it. The true fisherman uses a delicate pole, a delicate hook, a delicate bait, and he catches the fish. But you, not knowing better, take a weaver's beam, tie a rope to it, attach a pot-hook, bait with a scorpion, throw into the stream, and say, 'bite or be damned.' [Great laughter and applause.]

Let me say to all young folks there never was such a time to start out in life as now. Of all the ages, this is the best age there ever has been; of all the centuries, this is the best century; of all the decades of the century, this is the best decade; of all the years of the decade, this is the year; and of all the months of the year, this is the best month; and of all the days of the month, this is the best day. All the labor and experience of the ages have been expended to make the present moment possible. [Applause.]

We talk sometimes about the "good old times," but if we go back and see what they really did in those old days we shall find a state of things that would shock us to-day. We men are apt sometimes to talk about women's fashions, and to make fun of them, but there never was a time when the apparel of the women was as sensible and useful as it is to-day.   There was greater dissipation in the time of our fathers than there is to-day.   The wars to-day, even, are humane and Christian in comparison with the fearful combats and the slaughter of millions in the past.   The progress of history shows that the intelligent and Christian nations are increasing in numbers and power, and the ignorant and brutal are declining.   Spain once owned an eighth of the globe; now only a trifling fragment belongs to it.   The gold mines and the great strategic points of the world belong to the intelligent races, or race.   The Californias and Australias, India, Gibraltar, the Red Sea, the Cape of Good Hope, and the dominion of the sea belong to the Christian nations.   An intelligent nation reaches round the globe and gradually grasps power and extends the word of God. The most remarkable and useful inventions proceed from them, they make the soil more productive, and develop the resources of the earth.   There are men who talk about the danger of our being overrun by the Chinese, but when I hear a man talk that way I know he hasn't read history.   The world is being overrun by the civilized and enlightened people, not by the power of war, but by the arts of peace.   The world is better.

LESSON XXIII.

IS THE WORLD BETTER OR WORSE?—*Continued.*

The world has been revolutionized in the last fifty years. There were ages of darkness and struggling after light and liberty, but the nightmare began to pass away, and now in Europe, as well as our own continent, the people are free. There are some who think that Christianity is growing old, and the Bible has passed its day of usefulness. Aha! is that so? In all the centuries the number of Christians has been increasing, but in this nineteenth century statistics show that the increase has been greater than in any other that has ever passed, and greater than in all the other centuries that preceded it. In the eighteenth century there were two hundred million Christians; in the nineteenth century four hundred and fifty million Christians! [Applause.]

There never has been such a time to start out as now, because all the doors are opening. New Americas are being discovered. Columbus did not discover America— only the shell of it. Agassiz came and discovered fossiliferous America; Silliman discovered geological America; Longfellow discovered poetic America; and there are half a dozen other Americas yet to be discovered. Some of you, my young friends, will discover them. England for manufactures, Germany for scholarship, France for manners, but the United States for God. [Great applause.]

We have the best country in the world, and there are 850,000 fresh reasons for believing it; 850,000 people came in one year from other parts of the world to live in America. What did they come for? Because this is the best country in the world to live in. If it had not been, there would have been 850,000 Americans crossing the water to live elsewhere, for we know they are never satisfied until they find the very best place there is. We have everything that man could wish. If you do not find what you seek, don't stop at any one point and say there is no opening for you—because things are filled up, professions here and merchandise there, and this here and that there; go further and look out this land. We are just opening the outside doors of the wealth of this country. Pennsylvania coal for fires, Minnesota wheat for bread, fish from the Hudson and the Chattanooga, cotton from Mississippi, sugar from Louisiana, rice from the Carolinas for the queen of puddings, and poets and philosophers from Boston to explain to us all we ought to know [laughter], oats for the horses, carrots for the cattle, and oleomargarine for the hogs. [Renewed laughter and applause]. If you are nervous and feel strong go to the North; if your throats are delicate go to the South; if you feel crowded and want room go West; if you are tempted to become office-seekers go to jail. [Laughter.] There is place for every one, and that man ought not to live who can ever get the blues in this glorious country of ours. There are 36,000,000 people in France, but Texas is larger than France. The German empire has 47,000,000 people in it, yet Texas is larger than the empire.

Every way I look I see the world is brighter and growing better. All this new world in which we live is coming under one government. The nations at the south are gradually crumbling into our own; and then on the north, after awhile, the beautiful and hospitable Canada. To her the United States will offer heart and hand in marriage; and when our government shall offer its hand and heart to beautiful and hospitable Canada, Canada will blush and look down, and, thinking of her allegiance across the sea, will say, "Ask mother." [Great applause and laughter.] God will take possession of this fair country.

I need not talk to you of the public schools, where the children of the cord-wainer, the mechanic and glass-blower, sit side by side with the favorite sons of millionaires and merchant princes. Nor need I tell you of the asylums for the blind, the deaf and dumb, and the orphans, the widows, the outcasts. I thank God for the country of our residence; and while there are a thousand things that ought to be corrected and many wrongs that ought to be overthrown, I thank God for the past and look forward to a glorious future. I think we ought to toil with the sunlight in our faces. We are not fighting in a miserable Bull Run of defeat; we are on our way to final victory. We are not following the rider on the black horse, leading us down to death and darkness and doom, but the rider on the white horse, with the moon under his feet and the stars of Heaven for his tiara. Hail! Conqueror! Hail!

I know there are sorrows and there are sins and sufferings all about us; but as in some bitter, cold winter day

when we are threshing our arms around to keep our
thumbs from freezing, we think of the warm spring day
that after awhile will come; or in the dark winter nights
we look up and see the northern lights, the windows of
Heaven illuminated by some great victory; just so we see
a light streaming through from the other side, and we
know we are on the way to the morning—more than that,
to "a morning without clouds."

So the morning is coming to all the downtrodden
people. In Spain light is breaking over the Pyrenees, in
Italy it comes over the Alps, and in India over the Him-
alayas. The morning cometh, and the earth shall be filled
with its brightness. The advance of the ages is like the
rising of the tide. The waves come in and then recoil,
and we think the ocean is receding; but no, the tide rises.
The next wave rises higher, and the next higher and still
higher, and the tide is full and the earth is filled with the
glory of God as the waters cover the sea.

I never had such a realization of the greatness of our
country as came to me in one supreme, wonderful day—a
day which some others before me may remember—when I
stood in Washington after the war was over and watched
the army coming home. On they marched, down Pennsylvania Avenue, rank after rank, regiment after regiment,
battery following battery, horsemen and footmen, division
and army corps in long, unbroken line, their steady tramp,
tramp, tramp continuing for two whole days. We stood
and looked at them till the eye grew weary of banner and
plume and the rows of bayonets that flashed in the sun like
a river of silver, or, in the changing light, seemed to fill

all the streets with fire. We watched till the brain grew dizzy and the heart numb with the sight, and we had to avert our eyes, but still the tramp, tramp, tramp sounded in our ears to show that the pageant was going on. There was not a man whose eyes were not wet with weeping as we thought of the hardships and suffering which their marching meant, and of the brave men left behind in the sleep of the battle-field. Hush! all heads were uncovered—ten men left out of a whole regiment marched by, and tears of widows and orphans seemed to echo in their footsteps. But still they came, as if in never ending succession, from under the shadow of the Capitol. These were in the battles of the wilderness; those rode to victory behind the cavalry of Sheridan; another army marched with Sherman to the sea. I seem still to see that vast host marching on, company front, rank after rank, shoulder to shoulder, forward, and still forward, and I join in the cheers of those who welcome the warriors returning from the field of honor to the house of peace, for there was no North, no South, no East, no West, but everywhere was home—God's country for us all. [Prolonged applause].

LESSON XXIV.

REMARKS BY SENATOR SHERMAN IN FANUEIL HALL.

Mr. Chairman: It was with great hesitation that I accepted the invitation to speak here in this famous hall, this cradle of liberty, whose foundation was laid before the birth of American Independence, and whose completed walls echoed the eloquence of generations of men long before the state in which I live had a name or a place on the map of the world. I wish, in response to the invitation which has been given me, to recall to the attention and to the memory of the people of Massachusetts the origin of the great questions that divide the political parties of this country, and to give you, from the memories of the past, and from the recollections of two generations of great men in Massachusetts, the honest reasons why we people of Ohio come back to you and ask you to stand by the doctrines of your fathers.

I am among those who were taught in the school of politics and philosophy to believe that this country of ours was a great nation, a national government, and not a confederate government. I have been taught to believe that I am a citizen of the United States, and not a citizen of Ohio. I believe that we are bound to each by ties of allegiance and duty, so that I, though living remote from you, am akin to you, and bound by these ties of allegiance and duty to obey the laws of our country. I believe that the Constitution of the United States was framed by the people of the United States, and not by the states; that the states were merely used as a medium of gathering the will of the people, and that this government of ours is a government of the people, and by the people.

We recognize the high importance of the States of the Union; we give to those states our love as we would to a mother; but it is to the National Government we owe our paramount allegiance, and it is the Constitution of the United States that is the supreme law of the United States, which every man claiming to be an American citizen must obey, whether he lives in a state, new or old, or in a territory of the United States, or is on the high seas under the flag of the United States. My countrymen, this country is ours—yours and mine—and we are common inheritants of the greatest gifts that were ever given to the people in the wide world. Liberty and union, one and inseparable, now and forever, is the motto of the people of Ohio.

EXTRACT FROM AN ARGUMENT BY DANIEL WEBSTER.

Against the prisoner at the bar, as an individual, I can not have the slightest prejudice. I would not do him the smallest injury or injustice. But I do not affect to be indifferent to the discovery and the punishment of this deep guilt. I cheerfully share in the opprobrium, how muchsoever it may be, which is cast on those who feel and manifest anxious concern that all who had a part in the planning,

(8

or a hand in the executing, this deed of midnight assassination may be brought to answer for their enormous crime
at the bar of public justice.

Gentlemen, this is the most extraordinary case.   In
some respects it has hardly a precedent anywhere—certainly none in our New England history.   An aged man,
without an enemy in the world, in his own house, and in
his own bed, is made the victim of a butcherous murder,
for mere pay.   Deep sleep had fallen on the destined
victim and all beneath his roof.   A healthful old man, to
whom sleep was sweet; the first sound slumbers of the
night hold him to their soft but strong embrace.   The
assassin enters through the window, already prepared,
into an unoccupied apartment; with noiseless foot he paces
the lonely hall, half alighted by the moon; he winds up
the ascent of the stairs and reaches the door of the
chamber.   Of this he moves the lock, by soft and continued pressure, until it turns on its hinges, and he enters
and beholds his victim before him.   The room was uncommonly light.   The face of the innocent sleeper was turned
from the murderer, and the beams of the moon, resting on
the gray locks of his aged temple, showed him where to
strike.   The fatal blow was given, and the victim passes,
without a struggle or motion, from the repose of sleep to
the repose of death.   It is the assassin's purpose to make
sure work, and he yet plies the dagger, though it was
obvious that life had been destroyed by the blow of the
bludgeon.   He even raises the aged arm, that he may not
fail in his aim at the heart, and replaces it again over the

wound of the poniard. To finish the picture, he explores the wrist for the pulse. He feels for it, and ascertains that it beats no longer. It is accomplished; the deed is done. He retreats, retraces his steps to the window, passes through as he came in, and escapes. He has done the murder; no eye has seen him; no ear has heard him; the secret is his own, and it is safe. Ah, gentlemen, that was a dreadful mistake. Such a secret can be safe nowhere. The whole creation of God has neither nook nor corner where the guilty can bestow it and say it is safe. Not to speak of that eye which glances through all disguises and beholds everything as in the splendor of the noon—such secrets of guilt are never safe. "Murder will out." True it is that Providence so ordained, and doth so govern things, that those who break the great law of Heaven by shedding man's blood seldom succeed in avoiding dis- covery. Especially in a case exciting so much attention as this, discovery must, and will, come sooner or later. A thousand eyes turn at once to explore every man, every thing, every circumstance connected with the time and place; a thousand ears catch every whisper; a thousand excited minds intently dwell on the scene, shedding all their light, and ready to kindle the slightest circumstance into a blaze of discovery. Meantime the guilty soul can not keep its own secret. It is false to itself, or rather it feels an irresistible impulse of conscince; it labors under its guilty possession and knows not what to do with it. The human heart was not made for the residence of such an inhabitant; it finds itself preyed on by a torment which it dares not acknowledge to God or man. A vulture is devouring it, and it asks no sympathy or assistance either from Heaven or earth. The secret which the murderer possesses soon comes to possess him, and, like the evil spirit of which we read, it overcomes him and leads him whithersoever it will. He feels it beating at his heart, rising to his throat and demanding disclosure. He thinks the whole world sees it in his face, reads it in his eyes, and almost hears its workings in the very silence of his thoughts. It becomes his master; it betrays his discretion; it breaks down his courage; it conquers his prudence. When suspicions from without begin to embarrass him, and the net of circumstances to entangle him, the fatal secret struggles with still greater violence to burst forth. It must be confessed; it will be confessed; there is no refuge from confession but in suicide, and suicide is confession.

LESSON XXV.

___

SPEECH OF PATRICK HENRY

BEFORE THE VIRGINIA CONVENTION.

Mr. President : It is natural to man to indulge 'in the illusions of hope. We are apt to shut our eyes against a painful truth and listen to the song of that siren till she transforms us into beasts. Is this the part of wise men, engaged in a great and arduous struggle for liberty? Are we disposed to be of the number of those who, having eyes, see not, and having ears, hear not, the things which so nearly concern their temporal salvation? For my part, whatever anguish of spirit it may cost, I am willing to know the whole truth; to know the worst, and to provide for it.

I have but one lamp by which my feet are guided, and that is the lamp of experience. I know of no way of judging of the future but by the past. And judging by the past, I wish to know what there has been in the conduct of the British ministry for the last ten years to justify those hopes with which the gentlemen have been pleased to solace themselves and the House. Is it that insidious smile with which our petition has been lately received? Trust it not, sir; it will prove a snare to your feet. Suffer not yourselves to be betrayed by a kiss. Ask yourselves how this gracious reception of our petition comports with those warlike preparations which cover our waters and darken our land. Are fleets and armies necessary to a work of love and reconciliation? Have we shown ourselves so unwilling to be reconciled, that force must be called in to win back our love? Let us not deceive ourselves, sir. These are the implements of war and subjugation; the last arguments to which kings resort. I ask, gentlemen, what means this martial array, if its purpose be not to force us to submission? Can the gentlemen assign any other possible motive for it? Has Great Britian any enemy in this quarter of the world to call for all this accumulation of navies and armies? No, sir, she has none. They are meant for us; they can be meant for no other. They are sent over to bind and rivet upon us those chains which the British ministry have been so long forging. And what have we to oppose them? Shall we try argument? Sir, we have been trying that for the last ten years. Have we any-thing new to offer upon the subject? Nothing. We have held the subject up in every light of which it is capable; but it has been all in vain. Shall we resort to entreaty and humble supplication? What terms shall we find which have not been already exhausted? Let us not, I beseech you, deceive ourselves longer. Sir, we have done everything that could be done to avert the storm which is now coming on. We have petitioned; we have remon-strated; we have supplicated; we have prostrated ourselves before the throne, and have implored its interposition to arrest the tyrannical hands of the ministry and Parliament.

Our petitions have been slighted; our remonstrances have produced additional violence and insult; our supplications have been disregarded, and we have been spurned with contempt from the foot of the throne. In vain, after these things, may we indulge the fond hope of peace and reconciliation. *There is no longer any room for hope.* If we wish to be free; if we mean to preserve inviolate those inestimable privileges for which we have been so long contending; if we mean not basely to abandon the noble struggle in which we have been so long engaged, and which we have pledged ourselves never to abandon, until the glorious object of our contest shall be obtained; we must fight! I repeat it, sir, we must fight! An appeal to arms and to the God of hosts is all that is left us.

They tell us, sir, that we are weak; unable to cope with so formidable an adversary. But when shall we be stronger? Will it be next week or next year? Will it be when we are totally disarmed, and when a British guard shall be stationed in every house? Shall we gather strength by irresolution and inaction? Shall we acquire the means of effectual resistance by lying supinely on our backs and hugging the delusive phantom of hope, until our enemies shall have bound us hand and foot? Sir, we are not weak, if we make a proper use of those means which the God of nature hath placed in our power. Three millions of people, armed in the holy cause of liberty, and in such a country as that which we possess, are invincible by any force which our enemey can send against us. Besides, sir, we shall not fight our battles alone. There is a just God, who presides over the destinies, of nations, and who will raise up friends to fight our battles for us. The battle, sir, is not to the strong alone; it is to the vigilant, the active, the brave. Besides, sir, we have no election; if we were base enough to desire it, it is now too late to retire from the contest. There is no retreat but in submission and slavery. Our chains are forged.. Their clanking may be heard on the plains of Boston. The war is inevitable; and let it come! I repeat it, sir, let it come!

It is vain, sir, to extenuate the matter. Gentlemen may cry, Peace, peace; but there is no peace. The war is actually begun. The next gale that sweeps from the North will bring to our ears the clash of resounding arms. Our brethren are already in the field. Why stand we here idle? What is it that gentlemen wish? What would they have? Is life so dear, or peace so sweet, as to be purchased at the price of chains and slavery? Forbid it, Almighty God! I know not what course others may take; but, as for me, give me liberty, or give me death!

LESSON XXVI.

EXTRACTS FROM SPEECH

Delivered by Henry W. Grady before the Boston
Banquet, December 12, 1889.

Mr. President: Bidden by your invitation to a discussion of the race problem, forbidden by occasion to make a
political speech, I appreciate, in trying to reconcile order
with propriety, the perplexity of the little maid, who,
bidden to learn to swim, was yet adjured :

> " Now, go, my darling daughter,
>   Hang your clothes on a hickory limb,
>   And don't go near the water."

The stoutest apostle of the church, they say, is the missionary ; and the missionary, wherever he unfurls his flag,
will never find himself in deeper need of unction and
address than I, bidden to-night to plant the standard of a
southern Democrat in Boston's banquet hall, and to discuss the problem of the races in the home of Phillips and
of Sumner. But, Mr. President, if a purpose to speak in
perfect frankness and sincerity; if earnest understanding
of the vast interests involved; if a consecrating sense of
what disaster that must follow further misunderstanding

and estrangement; if these may be counted to steady un-disciplined speech and to strengthen an untried arm—then, sir, I shall find the courage to proceed.

Happy am I that this mission has brought my feet, at last, to press New England's historic soil, and my eyes to the knowledge of her beauty and her thrift. Here, within touch of Plymouth Rock and Bunker Hill—where Web-ster thundered and Longfellow sang, Emerson thought and Channing preached—here, in the cradle of American letters and almost of American liberty, I hasten to make the obeisance that every American owes New England when first he stands uncovered in her mighty presence. Strange apparition! This stern and unique figure—carved from the ocean and the wilderness—its majesty kindling and growing amid the storms of winters and wars, until at last the gloom was broken, its beauty disclosed in the tranquil sunshine, and the heroic workers rested at its base; while startled kings and emperors gazed and marveled that from the rude touch of this handful, cast on a bleak and unknown shore, should have come the embodied genius of human government and the perfect model of human liberty! God bless the memory of those immortal workers, and prosper the fortunes of their living sons, and perpetuate the inspiration of their handiwork!

Two years ago, sir, I spoke some words in New York that caught the attention of the North. As I stand here to reiterate and emphasize, as I have done everywhere, every word I then uttered—to declare that the sentiments I then avowed were universally approved in the South—

I realize that the confidence begotten by that speech is largely responsible for my presence here to-night. I should dishonor myself if I betrayed that confidence by uttering one insincere word, or by withholding one essential element of the truth.

Far to the south, Mr. President, separated from this section by a line—once defined in irrepressible difference, once traced in fratricidal blood, and now, thank God, but a vanishing shadow—lies the fairest and richest domain of this earth. It is the home of a brave and hospitable people. There, is centered all that can please or prosper mankind. A perfect climate above a fertile soil yields to the husbandman every product of the temperate zone. There, by night, the cotton whitens beneath the stars, and by day the wheat locks the sunshine in its bearded sheaf. In the same field the clover steals the fragrance of the wind, and the tobacco catches the quick aroma of the rains. There, are mountains stored with exhaustless treasures ; forests, vast and primeval; and rivers, that, tumbling or loitering, run wanton to the sea. Of three essential items of all industries—cotton, iron and wood—that region has easy control. In cotton, a fixed monopoly; in iron, proven supremacy; in timber, the reserve supply of the Republic. From this assured and permanent advantage, against which artificial conditions can not long prevail, has grown an amazing system of industries. Not maintained by human contrivance of tariff or capital, afar off from the fullest and cheapest source of supply, but resting in divine assurance, within touch of field and mine and forest—not set amid bleak hills and costly farms from which competition has driven the farmer in despair, but amid cheap and sunny lands, rich with agriculture, to which neither season nor soil has set a limit—this system of industries is mounting to a splendor that shall dazzle and illumine the world.   That, sir, is the picture and the promise of my home—a land better and fairer than I have told you, and yet but fit setting, in its material excellence, for the loyal and gentle quality of its citizenship. Against that, sir, we have New England recruiting the Republic from its sturdy loins, shaking from its overcrowded hives new swarms of workers, and touching this land all over with its energy and its courage. And yet, while in the Eldorado of which I have told you but 15 per cent. of lands are cultivated, its mines scarcely touched, and its population so scant that, were it set equidistant, the sound of the human voice could not be heard from Virginia to Texas; while on the threshold of nearly every house in New England stands a son, seeking, with troubled eyes, some new land into which to carry his modest patrimony, and the homely training that is better than gold, the strange fact remains that in 1880 the South had fewer northern-born citizens than she had in 1870; fewer in 1870 than in 1860. Why is this? Why is it, sir, though the sectional line be now but a mist that the breath may dispel, that fewer men of the North have crossed it over to the South than when it was crimson with the best blood of the Republic, or even when the slave-holder stood guard over every inch of its way?

LESSON XXVII.

EXTRACTS FROM HENRY W. GRADY'S SPEECH—*Continued.*

There can be but one answer. It is the very problem we are now to consider. The key that opens that problem will unlock to the world the fairest half of this Republic, and free the halted feet of thousands whose eyes are already kindling with its beauty. Better than this, it will open the hearts of brothers for thirty years estranged, and clasp in lasting comradeship a million hands now withheld in doubt. Nothing, sir, but this problem, and the suspicion it breeds, hinders a clear understanding and a perfect union. Nothing else stands between us and such love as bound Georgia and Massachusetts at Valley Forge and Yorktown, chastened by the sacrifices of Manassas and Gettysburg, and illumined with the coming of better work and a nobler destiny than was ever wrought with the sword, or sought at the cannon's mouth.

If this does not invite your patient hearing to-night, hear one thing more. My people, your brothers in the South—brothers in blood, in destiny, in all that is best in our past and future—are so beset with this problem that their very existence depends on its right solution. Nor are they wholly to blame for its presence. The slave-ships of the Republic sailed from your ports; the slaves

worked in our fields. You will not defend the traffic, nor
I the institution. But I do here declare that in its wise
and humane administration, in lifting the slave to heights
of which he had not dreamed in his savage home, and
giving him a happiness he has not yet found in freedom,
our fathers left their sons a saving and excellent heritage.
In the storm of war this institution was lost. I thank
God as heartily as you do that human slavery is gone forever from American soil. But the freedman remains;
with him a problem without precedent or parallel. Note
its appalling conditions: Two utterly dissimilar races on
the same soil, with equal political and civil rights,
almost equal in numbers, but terribly unequal in intelligence and responsibility; each pledged against fusion;
one for a century in servitude to the other, and freed at
last by a desolating war; the experiment sought by
neither, but approached by both with doubt; these are
the conditions. Under these, adverse at every point, we
are required to carry these two races in peace and honor
to the end.

Never, sir, has such a task been given to mortal stew-
ardship. Never before in this Republic has the white race
divided on the right of an alien race. The red man was
cut down as a weed, because he hindered the way of the
American citizen. The yellow man was shut out of this
Republic because he is an alien and inferior. The red
man was owner of the land; the yellow man highly civilized and assimilable; but they hindered both sections, and
are gone! But the black man, clothed with every privi-

lege of government, affecting but one section, is pinned to
the soil, and my people commanded to make good, at any
hazard, and at any cost, his full and equal heirship of
American privilege and prosperity. It matters not that
every other race has been routed or excluded, without rhyme
or reason. It matters not that wherever the whites and
blacks have touched, in any era or in any clime, there has
been irreconcilable violence. It matters not that no two
races, however similar, have ever lived anywhere, at any
time, on the same soil with equal rights in peace! In
spite of these things we are commanded to make good
this change of American policy which has not, perhaps,
changed American prejudice; to make certain here
what has elsewhere been impossible between whites and
blacks; and to reverse, under the very worst conditions,
the universal verdict of racial history; and driven, sir, to
this superhuman task with an impatience that brooks no
delay, a rigor that accepts no excuse, and a suspicion that
discourages frankness and sincerity. We do not shrink
from this trial. It is so interwoven with our industrial
fabric that we can not disentangle it if we would—so bound
up in our honorable obligation to the world that we
would not if we could. Can we solve it? The God who
gave it into our hands, He alone can know. But this, the
weakest and wisest of us do know: We can not solve it
with less than your tolerant and patient sympathy; with
less than the knowledge that the blood that runs in your
veins is our blood, and that, when we have done our best,
whether the issue be lost or won, we shall feel your strong

arms about us and hear the beating of your approving hearts!

The resolute, clear-headed, broad-minded men of the South—the men whose genius made glorious every page of the first seventy years of American history, whose courage and fortitude you tested in five years of the fiercest war, whose energy has made bricks without straw, and spread splendor amid the ashes of their war-wasted homes—these men wear this problem in their hearts and their brains by day and by night. They realize, as you can not, what this problem means; what they owe to this kindly and dependent race; the measure of their debt to the world in whose despite they defended and maintained slavery. And though their feet are hindered in its undergrowth, and their march cumbered with its burdens, they have lost neither the patience from which comes clearness nor the faith from which comes courage. Nor, sir, when in passionate moments is disclosed to them that vague and awful shadow, with its lurid abysses, and its crimson stains, into which I pray God they may never go, are they struck with more apprehension than is needed to complete their consecration!

LESSON XXVIII.

EXTRACTS FROM HENRY W. GRADY'S SPEECH—*Continued.*

Such is the temper of my people. But what of the problem itself? Mr. President, we need not go one step further unless you concede right here that the people I speak for are as honest, as sensible, and as just, as your people; seeking as earnestly as you would in their place, to rightly solve a problem that touches them at every vital point. If you insist that they are ruffians, blindly striving with bludgeon and shot-gun to plunder and oppress a race, then I shall tax your patience in vain. But admit that they are men of common sense and common honesty, wisely modifying an environment they can not wholly disregard, guiding and controlling as best they can the vicious and irresponsible of either race, compensating error with frankness, and retrieving in patience what they lose in passion, and conscious all the time that wrong means ruin—admit this, and we may reach an understanding to-night.

I bespeak your patience while, with rigorous plainness of speech seeking your judgment rather than your applause, I proceed step by step. We give to the world this year a crop of 7,500,000 bales of cotton, worth $450,-000,000, and its cash equivalent in grain, grasses and fruit. This enormous crop could not have come from the hands

(9)

of sullen and discontented labor. It comes from peaceful fields, in which laughter and gossip rise above the hum of industry, and contentment runs with the singing plow. It is claimed that this ignorant labor is defrauded of its just hire. I present the tax-books of Georgia, which show that the negro, twenty-five years ago a slave, has in Georgia alone $10,000,000 of assessed property, worth twice that much. Does not that record honor him, and vindicate his neighbors? What people, penniless, illiterate, has done so well? For every Afro-American agitator, stirring the strife in which alone he prospers, I can show you a hundred negroes, happy in their cabin homes, tilling their own land by day, and at night taking from the lips of their children the helpful message their state sends them from the school-house door. And the school-house itself bears testimony. In Georgia we added last year $250,000 to the school fund, making a total of more than $1,000,000; and this in the face of prejudice not yet conquered—of the fact that the whites are assessed for $368,000,000, the blacks for $10,000,000, and yet 49 per cent. of the beneficiaries are black children, and in the doubt of many wise men if education helps or can help our problem. Charleston, with her taxable values cut half in two since 1860, pays more in proportion for public schools than Boston. Although it is easier to give much out of much than little out of little, the South, with one-seventh of the taxable property of the country, with relatively larger debt, having received only one-twelfth as much of public lands, and having back of its tax-books

none of the half-billion of bonds that enrich the North,
yet gives nearly one-sixth of the public-school fund. The
South since 1865 has spent $122,000,000 in education, and
this year is pledged to $37,000,000 more for state and city
schools, although the blacks, paying one-thirtieth of the
taxes, get nearly one-half of the fund. Go into our fields
and see whites and blacks working side by side; on our
buildings in the same squad; in our shops at the same
forge. Often the blacks crowd the whites from work, or
lower wages by their greater need or simpler habits, and
yet are permitted, because we want to bar them from no
avenue in which their feet is fitted to tread. They could
not there be elected orators of white universities, as they
have been here; but they do enter there a hundred useful
trades that are closed against them here. We hold it
better and wiser to tend the weeds in the garden than to
water the exotic in the window. In the South there are
negro lawyers, teachers, editors, dentists, doctors, preach-
ers, working in peace and multiplying with the increasing
ability of their race to support them. In villages and
towns they have their military companies equipped from
the armories of the state, their churches and societies built
and supported largely by their neighbors. What is the
testimony of the courts? In penal legislation we have
steadily reduced felonies to misdemeanors, and have led
the world in mitigating punishment for crime, that we
might save, as far as possible, this dependent race from its
own weakness. In our penitentiary record 60 per cent.
of the prosecutors are negroes, and in every court the

negro criminal strikes the colored juror, that white men may judge his case. In the North, one negro in every 185 is in jail; in the South, only one in 446. In the North the percentage of negro prisoners is six times as great as that of native whites; in the South, only four times as great. If prejudice wrongs him in southern courts, the record shows it to be deeper in northern courts. I assert here, and a bar as intelligent and upright as the bar of Massachusetts will solemnly indorse my assertion, that in the southern courts, from highest to lowest, pleading for either liberty or property, the negro has distinct advantage, because he is a negro, apt to be overreached, oppressed, and that this advantage reaches from the juror in making his verdict to the judge measuring his sentence. Now, Mr. President, can it be seriously maintained that we are terrorizing the people from whose willing hands comes every year $1,000,000,000 of farm crops? Or have robbed a people who, twenty-five years from unrewarded slavery, have amassed in one state $20,000,000 of property? Or that we intend to oppress the people we are arming every day? Or deceive them, when we are educating them to the utmost limit of our ability? Or outlaw them, when we work side by side with them? Or re-enslave them under legal forms, when for their benefit we have even imprudently narrowed the limit of felonies and mitigated the severity of law? My fellow-countryman, as yourself may sometime have to appeal at the bar of human judgment for justice and for right, give to my people to-night the fair and unanswerable conclusion of these incontestable facts!

LESSON XXIX.

EXTRACTS FROM HENRY W. GRADY'S SPEECH—*Continued.*

I regret, sir, that my section, hindered with this problem, can not align itself—stands in seeming estrangement to the North. If, sir, any man will point out to me a path down which the white people of the South, divided, may walk in peace and honor, I will take that path, though I take it alone; for at its end, and nowhere else, I fear, is to be found the full prosperity of my section, and the full restoration of this Union. But, sir, if the negro had not been enfranchised the South would have been divided and the Republic united. His enfranchisement—against which I enter no protest—holds the South united and compact. What solution can we offer for the problem? Time alone can disclose it to us. I simply report progress and ask your patience. If the problem be solved at all—and I firmly believe it will, though nowhere else has it been— it will be solved by the people most deeply bound in interest, most deeply pledged in honor to its solution. I would rather see my people render back this question rightly solved, than to see them gather all the spoils over which faction has contended since Cataline conspired and Cæsar fought. Meantime we treat the negro fairly, measuring to him justice in the fulness the strong should give to the weak, and leading him in the steadfast ways of citzenship that he may no longer be the prey of the unscrupulous and the sport of the thoughtless. We open to him every pursuit in which he can prosper, and seek to broaden his training and capacity. We seek to hold his confidence and friendship, and to pin him to the soil with ownership, that he may catch in the fire of his own hearthstone that sense of responsibility the shiftless can never know.

And we gather him into that alliance of property and knowledge that though it runs close to racial lines, welcomes the responsible and intelligent of any race. By this course, confirmed in our judgment and justified in the progress already made, we hope to progress slowly but surely to the end.

Whatever the future may hold for them, whether they plod along in the servitude from which they have never been lifted since the Cyrenian was laid hold upon by the Roman soldiers and made to bear the cross of the fainting Christ; whether they find homes again in Africa, and thus hasten the prophecy of the psalmist who said : " And suddenly Ethiopia shall hold out her hands unto God "; whether forever dislocated and separate, they remain a weak people, beset by stronger, and exist as the Turk, who lives in the jealousy rather than in the conscience of Europe; or whether, in this miraculous Republic, they break through the caste of twenty centuries, and belying universal history, reach the full stature of citizenship and in peace maintain it, we shall give them uttermost justice and abiding friendship. And whatever we do, into whatever seeming estrangement we may be driven, nothing shall disturb the love we bear this Republic or mitigate our consecration to its service. I stand here, Mr. President, to profess no new loyalty. When General Lee, whose heart was the temple of our hopes and whose arm was clothed with our strength, renewed his allegiance to this government at Appomatox he spoke from a heart too great to be false, and he spoke for every honest man from Maryland to Texas. From that day to this, Hamilcar has nowhere in the South sworn young Hannibal to hatred and vengeance, but everywhere to loyalty and to love. Witness the veteran standing at the base of a Confederate monument, above the graves of his comrades, his empty sleeve tossing in the April wind, adjuring the young men about him to serve as earnest and loyal citizens the government against which their fathers fought. This message, delivered from that sacred presence, has gone home to the hearts of my fellows. And, sir, I declare here, if physical courage be always equal to human aspiration, that they would die, sir, if need be, to restore this Republic their fathers sought to dissolve.

Such, Mr. President, is this problem as we see it, such the temper in which we approach it, such the progress made. What do we ask of you? First, patience; out of this alone can come perfect work. Second, confidence; in this alone can you judge fairly. Third, sympathy; in this you can help us best. Fourth, loyalty to the Republic; for there is sectionalism in loyalty as in estrangement. This hour little needs the loyalty that is loyal to one section and yet holds the other in enduring suspicion and estrangement. Give us the broad and perfect loyalty that loves and trusts Georgia alike with Massachusetts; that knows no South, no North, no East, no West; but endears with equal and patriotic love every foot of our soil, every state of our Union.

A mighty duty, sir, and a mighty inspiration impels every one of us to-night to lose in patriotic consecration whatever estranges, whatever divides. We, sir, are Americans, and we fight for human liberty ! . The uplifting force of the American idea is under every throne on earth. France, Brazil, these are our victories. To redeem the earth from kingcraft and oppression, that is our mission. And we shall not fail. God has sown in our soil the seed of His millennial harvest, and He will not lay the sickle to the ripening crop until His full and perfect day has come. Our history, sir, has been a constant and expanding miracle, from Plymouth rock and Jamestown all the way; aye, even from the hour when, from the voiceless and trackless ocean, a new world rose to the sight of the inspired sailor. As we approach the fourth centennial of that stupendous day, when the Old World will come to marvel and to learn amid our gathered treasures, let us resolve to crown the miracles of our past with the spectacle of a Republic compact, united, indissoluble in the bonds of love; loving from the lakes to the gulf, the wounds of war healed in every heart as on every hill; serene and resplendent at the summit of human achievement and earthly glory, blazing out the path and making clear the way up which all the nations of the earth must come in God's appointed time!

LESSON XXX.

COURT PROCEEDINGS.

COUNTY COURT—Allegany County.

MARIA EVANS vs. J. G. DENNING.	Before Hon. Clarence Farnum and a Jury.

APPEARANCES:

For the Plaintiff—Mr. Van Fleet.
For the Defendant—Mr. H. W. Norton.

Proceedings May 10, 1883.

The Plaintiff stated his case to the Jury.

Levi Evans, sworn on behalf of the plaintiff, testified as follows:

Q. You are the husband of the plaintiff in this case ? A. Yes, sir.

Q. You are acquainted with the defendant? A. Yes, sir ; I know him.

Q. You may examine that note.

(Paper handed to witness.)

Q. Was there a time when you went to Fremont and presented that note to the defendant? A. Yes, sir.

Q. When was that? A. That was in December, I think.

Q. December of what year? A. In 1879.

Q. You may state whether he admitted the execution of that note? A. He did.

Q. Was the note then in its present condition? A. Yes, sir; it was.

Mr. Van Fleet: I now offer the note in evidence again.

Mr. Norton: I will cross examine first.

Cross examination by Mr. Norton:

Q. You say it was in December, 1879. A. I think it was.

Q. When you were at Fremont? A. Yes, sir.

Q. What did you go there for? A. To get some money.

Q. On this note? A. Yes, sir.

Q. You had the note with you when you went there? A. Yes, sir.

Q. Where did you first see him after you went there? A. Well, I think he was in the office; I saw him going across from the house, but I think the first I spoke to him was in his office over at the house.

Q. Now, when did you first show him the note after you got there? A. I didn't show it to him until after he and I made up a statement.

Q. You and he figured some before you showed him the note? A. Yes, sir.

Q. You testified when Mr. Van Fleet asked you about it, that he admitted the execution of the note, and was going to pay it. A. He said he signed the note and was going to pay it.

Q. Now wasn't there some talk between you and Mr. Denning at that time about the note being for $75 or $150? A. No, sir; there wasn't a word said about the note; what it was for.

Q. Did he look at the note? A. That day?

Q. Yes, sir. A. Yes, sir.

Q. Now while you were there that day, he offered to pay you some money on the note, did he not? A. Yes, sir; he offered to pay me some money.

Q. Now while he was there was this indorsement written on this note "received on the within, $39.94." A. Yes, sir.

Mr. Van Fleet: To that I object.

The Court: I think perhaps we are entitled to have all there was of it.

Mr. Van Fleet: You don't take it as evidence of payment?

The Court: No.

Q. Now after he had written that upon there—$39.94 —that was written in your presence was it not? A. Yes, sir.

Q. That indorsement was dated June 6, 1879, I think. A. But it was put on in December.

Q. It was put on at the time you were there in December? A. Yes, sir.

Q. But there was a talk there of something having been paid, and that was put on?   A. Yes, sir.

Q. Now at that time—when he offered to pay you— you consented that this should be put on, and he was to pay you the balance of the amount on the note?   A. Will you allow me to tell what was said?

Q. No, sir; you answer my question.   You consented that he should put this on and then he was going to pay you the balance?   A. No, sir; that was not the way of it.

Q. As a matter of fact after this was put on he offered to pay you something—about $40.00 or more?   A. No, sir.

Q. How much was it he offered to pay you?   A. He said he had $32.00, but he would not let me take it and count it.

Q. He offered to pay you $32.00 if you would take it and accept it?   A. He offered me a roll of money, but he would not let me take it and count it.

Q. He offered you some money which he said was about $32.00, and you wouldn't accept it?   A. Yes, sir.

Q. You claimed it should be more?   A. Yes, sir.

Q. Now $32.00 in addition to this $39.34 would have been sufficient to have paid the amount due you on this note, wouldn't it?   A. Why I presume if that had been put on there for a payment.

Q. Well, $32.00, whatever he offered you in addition to what was indorsed on here, would have been enough to have paid this note?   A. Forty dollars and $32.00 being $72.00.

Q. Did he say he would pay you $32.00, or was it about $38.00 that he offered you. A. No, sir; he didn't say $38.00 at all, he said $32.00.

Q. Now when did you first see this note? A. I saw it, I should think, between the 15th and the 20th of May.

Q. You were sworn upon. a previous trial, were you not? A. Yes, sir

Q. Did you swear upon that trial that when you saw that note, at that time, these alterations had not been made? A. No, sir.

Q. You did not swear to that on that trial? A. No, sir.

Q. If you should see it written out here, where you had sworn to it, would you think you did it? A. No, sir; I would not.

Q. You were acting as agent for you wife? A. Yes, sir.

Q. Now at the same time when you were up there to Dr. Dunning's, did you also go down to Mr. Maynard's? A. Yes, sir.

Q. And you had some talk there? A. Yes, sir.

Re-direct examination by Mr. Van Fleet:

Q. I understood you to say that he had this note in his hands and made this indorsement upon its back? A. Yes, sir; in December after I was there.

Q. And he admitted its execution after an examination of it? A. Yes, sir.

Mr. Norton: What did he say about admitting its execution? A. He said he signed all of those notes.

Q. There were several others spoken of? A. All of those cheese notes.

Mr. Van Fleet: And he did not say anything about any alterations in the note? A. No, sir; he did not.

Mr. Van Fleet: I now read the note in evidence:

$75.00.   *May 14th, 1875.*

For value received we jointly and severally agree to pay Maria Evans seventy-five dollars, sixty days from date.

C. C. DENNING.

J. G. DENNING.

Mr. Van Fleet: That is our case.

Plaintiff rests.

Mr. Norton: The defendant moves for a non-suit upon the ground that the plaintiff has not proved facts sufficient to concede cause of action; that there is a fatal variance between the complaint and the proof; that the complaint asks and demands judgment on a note for $150.00, describing it, while the note offered in evidence is a note for $75.00; and also upon the further ground that there have been material alterations in the note which it does not appear were made with the consent of the defendant.

Motion denied, and exception.

LESSON XXXI.

COURT PROCEEDINGS—*Continued.*

Dr. C. C. DENNING, defendant, sworn and examined by Mr. Norton, testifies as follows:

Q. Where do you reside?   A. Fremont.

Q. What is your occupation?   A. Physician and surgeon.

Q. How long have you lived there?   A. Fourteen years.

Q. Where did this brother of yours reside?   A. Andover.

Q. This J. G. Denning was your brother?   A. Yes, sir.

Q. When did he die?   A. I think it was in September, 1879.

Q. Now, Doctor, you signed this note C. C. Denning did you?

(Note shown to witness.)

A. Yes, sir.

Q. When you signed that note was it in the same condition, and did it have the same appearance which it has now?   A. No, sir.

Q. What changes appear to have been made since you signed it?   A. The date of May 12 has been changed to May 14; in the body of the note a part of the seven has been erased and a cipher added to the right of the five.

Q. Those changes have been made since the note left your possession?　A. Yes, sir.

Q. Were they made with your knowledge or consent? A. No, sir.

Q. Did you ever give anybody such authority to make such changes?　A. No, sir.

Q. Doctor, what was the consideration to you upon this note?　A. There wasn't any.

Q. You merely signed it for accommodation?　A. Yes, sir.

Q. Now, when Mr. Evans came to your office, what was the conversation in there, that you recollect?　A. He told me he had come to settle up; I asked him if he had the note with him, and he said he had; I asked him to let me see it; I took the note and turned it over and looked at the back, and I said to him, there has been $40.00 paid on this note, hasn't there?　he said, yes, or about that; I said to him that this should have been indorsed on the note; I said to him, you indorse what has been paid on the note and I will either pay you the balance or give you my note, due in three weeks; he said, you indorse it and I will sign the name to the indorsement; I put on the indorsement and handed the note back to him; I went to father and borrowed the money and he hadn't then signed the name; I gave the money to Doctor Coller and said, when he signs that you can pay him.

Q. But you didn't notice the other alterations?　A. No, sir; not until afterwards.

Q. Did you ever intend in any way to write this note as it appears to be altered? No, sir.

Cross examination by Mr. Van Fleet:

Q. When did you first notice the alterations in the figures in the body of the note? A. I think it was at Andover during the first suit; I think Mr. Scott called my attention to the change in it at that time.

Q. Was there anything said at Andover in regard to the alterations? A. We put in no evidence that I know of.

Q. You had this note in your hands and looked at it, did you not? A. Yes, sir.

Q. When did you first know that Evans claimed to have a note for $150.00? A. I received a letter from Mrs. Evans claiming that she had a note for $150.00.

Q. Did you not claim to Evans that the note was given as security for sixty days milk?

Mr. Norton: I object to that, it is immaterial.

Objection overruled, and exception.

A. I think I told Evans that I signed that note with my brother.

Q. Did you not claim to Evans that the note was given as security for sixty days milk? A. Yes, sir.

Q. Now was there not a time when you got Mr. Evans with others at Andover to see about settling up? Yes, sir.

Q. You then ascertained the amount of milk your brother had received? A. Not at that time.

Q. Was there not a figuring up there at that time? A. No, sir.

(10)

Q. Did you not in the presence of this plaintiff's husband, Evans, and Aaron Kennedy and other patrons have a figuring up?   A. No, sir.

Q. When was it that you found out the amount of milk that Evans had?

Mr. Norton: Immaterial.

The Court: You claim there is no consideration for this?

Mr. Norton: We are not defending on that.

Mr. Van Fleet: It is simply material that he claimed at this time that the note was given as security for 60 days milk; he claimed that upon this note should be indorsed $40.00, and the amount of milk was there figured up, which was some 18,000 pounds of milk that remained unpaid for the first 60 days, and then there is further evidence that I don't like to state.

Objection overruled, exception taken.

Q. Did you not in September, the first time that you were there to meet the patrons, have a figuring of the amount of milk each patron had delivered to J. G. Denning, during the first 60 days, in the presence of Levi and Aaron Kennedy and other men?   A. No, sir.

Q. Nothing of the kind?   A. Nothing of the kind.

Re-direct examination by Mr. Norton:

Q. You say that your understanding was from Mr. Evans that this note was given to secure the first 60 days milk?   A. Yes, sir.

Q. That you had no interest in whatever?   A. No, sir.

Q. And whatever was paid, was to be indorsed on the note?   A. Yes, sir, that is the way I understood it.

LYMAN DENNING, sworn in behalf of the defendant, was examined by Mr. Norton, and testified as follows:

Q. You are the father of Mr. Denning, the defendant? A. Yes, sir.

Q. Were you present at the house of the Doctor in December, 1879, when Mr. Evans came there? A. I was there when he came there, and I think it was about that time, for I don't remember the dates particularly.

Q. Now when he came there, was there some talk about the note? A. There was some talk about it.

Q. You may state whether or not the Doctor asked him any questions about whether anything had been paid on the note? A. Well, he spoke about the note; I think Evans did and referred to the note, and the Doctor asked him if there had not been some paid on it, or if there was an indorsement on it, or something about that, and he said there was no indorsement, but that he had some money; I think as near as I can recollect it was $39.00

Q. The Doctor was asking him about the note at that time? A. Yes, sir.

Q. What was said about his indorsing this amount on this note, if any? A. He asked him to indorse it, and I think Evans told him to indorse it and he would sign it, and the Doctor indorsed it, I believe, and there was some talk about it afterwards; I think Evans refused to sign it.

Q. Well, now, was there some talk about the balance being paid there at that time, Mr. Denning? A. There was; the Doctor told him if he would make the indorsement that he would pay the balance of the note; that was the talk about the payment, I think.

Q. You may state whether or not any money was offered there? A. Well, the Doctor offered him some
money or gave it to Doctor Collier, I think his name was,
and he offered him the money, I think.

Q. Now do you know how much money it was the
Doctor had there and offered to pay, or about how much
it was? A. I think the Doctor said something about not
having enough to pay it in full, and I think I let him
have something like $32.00.

Q. Did you go with him when he went down to the
bank? A. I didn't.

Q. Did you see the note on that occasion? A. I didn't
have it in my hands.

Q. How old a man are you, Mr. Denning? A. 73.

LESSON XXXII.

COURT PROCEEDINGS—*Continued.*

Cross examination by Mr. Van Fleet:

Q. You may start in and tell all that you remember that was said there in the Doctor's office between Mr. Evans and the Doctor?   A. I don't think I could remember all that was said.

Q. Tell all that you remember.   A. The principal talk between them was with reference to what money Evans had had, and about the indorsement.

Q. Well, tell what was said; all that you can remember.   A. Well, the Doctor asked him if he hadn't had some money, and he said he had; and the Doctor spoke about whether it was indorsed on the note, or something to that effect, and he admitted that it was not on the note, and he said that he would indorse it on the note, what he had had, and he would pay him the balance of the note.

Q. Do you recollect anything else?   A. I don't know as I do particularly now.

Q. How long was Evans there in the office?   A. Well, I couldn't say as to that; I should think he might have been there an hour.

Q. And the note was there under debate during that time?   A. Well, I don't know as there was any particular debate about the note.

Q. Well, the note was there?   A. Yes, sir.

Q. Laid on the table?   A. I don't know as it laid there all the while.

Q. It laid there most of the time, did it not?   A. Well, I couldn't say as to that; couldn't be positive any further than that I think I saw the Doctor take it and write on it what I supposed was the note, from the conversation.

Q. Now do you recollect anything being said about milk there?   A. I don't know that I do.

MORRIS C. MAYNARD, sworn in behalf of the defendant, was examined by Mr. Norton, and testified as follows:

Q. Where do you reside?   A. Fremont.

Q. What is your occupation?   A. I am a banker.

Q. You know Mr. Denning?   A. Yes, sir.

Q. And you know this defendant?   A. I have seen him on one occasion before.

Q. Do you know the time when they came to your banking office?   A. Yes, sir.

Q. Who came?   A. This gentleman and Mr. Denning.

Q. You may state what occured while they were there. A. I think this gentleman came in first, and Mr. Denning immediately after him; I was there in my office and this gentleman said Dr. Denning says that he will pay me $110.00, and Dr. Denning said no, I didn't say any such thing; and the Doctor offered him somewhere between $37 and $38, and tendered it to him as the balance due on the note, and offered it to him two or three times while there as a tender on the note, and Evans refused to take it, claiming, I think, there was more due.

Q. Claiming the note was more? A. Yes, sir; and the money was then left in my hands as a tender for Evans when he called for it.

Q. Was anything said about the amount that was paid on the note? A. I think there was a talk there between them of $40.00, and I think there was about $40.00 indorsed on the note. Either I asked to see the note or the Doctor requested him to show me the note, and there was quite a hesitancy, and this man wouldn't let this note get out of his hands, nor didn't during the time it was there, and held it up so that I read it, and then looked on the back and saw the indorsement, but I did not ·know that I had hold of that note, if I did he had hold of the other end of it.

DOCTOR DENNING, recalled, examined by Mr. Norton:

Q. At the time Mr. Evans was up to your house, was the note lying on the table for any considerable time? A. Only just while I was indorsing it.

Q. What became of it after you indorsed it? A. I slid it back on the secretary, and he picked up the note.

Q. You gave the note no particular examination? A. No, sir.

Defendant rests.

MARIA EVANS, recalled for the plaintiff, and examined by Mr. Van Fleet:

Q. Were there ever any payments made on this note in question?

Mr. Norton: I object to that; it calls for a conclusion that the jury are to be judges of, the fact as to whether any payment has been made upon this note, and they have brought out the testimony quite fully in reference to this milk business.

Objection sustained, and exception taken.

(Paper shown to witness.)

Q. At the time the forty dollars was paid, or about forty dollars, you had that contract with J. G. Denning? A. Yes, sir; I had that contract.

Q. And the forty dollars was paid to you by J. G. Denning? A. He sent it over by a milkman.

Q. You acknowledged that it came from J. G. Denning? A. Yes, sir.

Cross examination by Mr. Norton:

Q. Did you also receive some cheese from J. G. Denning?

Mr. Van Fleet: To that I object; It is not admissible under the pleading.

Objection sustained, and exception.

Mr. Van Fleet: I now in connection with the testimony of Mr. Evans offer this book in evidence as the book which was figured on.

Mr. Norton: Immaterial, incompetent and inadmissible under the pleadings.

Objection sustained.

Mr. Norton: I understand that the erasure was made by you, Mr. Van Fleet, after the note came into your hands for collection, the indorsement on the back?

Mr. Van Fleet: That is conceded.

Plaintiff rests.

Doctor COLLIER, recalled by Mr. Norton:

You heard what Mr. Evans has said occurred at Mr. Dennings house?   A. Yes, sir.

Q. Did it occur as Mr. Evans said; was there anything different that you recollect occurred there from what you stated when you were on the stand?   A. No, sir.

Cross examined by Mr. Van Fleet:

Q. You don't recollect the whole transaction, you don't pretend to remember everything that occurred there?   A. I remember all the prominent features of the conversation while I was in the office, I think.

Testimony closed.

LESSON XXXIII.

TRIAL OF ANDREW JOHNSON,

BEFORE THE SENATE OF THE UNITED STATES, ON IM-
PEACHMENT BY THE HOUSE OF REPRESENTATIVES
FOR HIGH CRIMES AND MISDEMEANORS.

JAMES B. SHERIDAN, being duly sworn on behalf of
the appellants, testifies as follows:

Direct examination by Mr. Manager Butler, acting for
the House of Representatives:

Q. Your whole name, Mr. Sheridan? A. James
Bernard Sheridan.

Q. What is your business? A. I am a stenographer.

Q. Where employed? A. At present in New York
City.

Q. What was your business on the 18th of August,
1866? A. I was a stenographer.

Q. State whether you reported a speech of the President
on the 18th of August, 1866, in the east room of the
President's Mansion? A. I did.

Q. Have you the notes taken at the time of that speech?
A. I have (producing a note-book containing short-hand
notes).

Q. Did you take down that speech correctly as it was
given? A. I did, to the best of my ability.

Q. How long experience have you had as a reporter?
A. Some fourteen years now.

Q. Did you write out that speech at the time? A. I wrote out a part of it.

Q. Where? A. At the Presidential Mansion.

Q. Who was present? A. There were several reporters present—Mr. Clephane, Mr. Smith.

Q. What Clephane? Do you remember his first name? A. James, I think, is his first name.

Q. What Mr. Smith? A. Francis H., I believe, is his name.

Q. The official reporter of the House? At that time, I believe, he was connected with the House.

Q. Who else? A. I think Colonel Moore was in the room part of the time; I do not know that he was in all the time.

Q. What Colonel Moore? A. The President's private secretary, William G.

Q. After it was written out, what, if anything, was done with it?

Mr. Curtiss: He says he wrote a part.

Mr. Manager Butler: The part that you wrote out? A. I do not know; I think Mr. Moore took it; I was very sick at the time, and did not pay much attention to what was going on.

Q. You think Mr. Moore took it? A. I think either he or Mr. Smith took it, as I wrote out my share of it. We divided it among us; Mr. Clephane, Mr. Smith and I wrote out the speech, I think.

Q. Look at that manuscript (handing to the witness the manuscript produced by C. A. Tinker) and see whether you recognize your handwriting?

The witness (having examined the manuscript): No, sir; I do not recognize any of the writing here as mine.

Q. Have you since written out from your notes any portion of the speech as you reported it? A. I wrote out a couple of extracts from it.

Q. (Handing a paper to witness.) Is that your writing? A. Yes, sir.

Q. State whether what you hold in your hand is a correct transcript of that speech made from your notes? A. It is.

Q. When was that written? A. It was written when I appeared before the Board of Managers.

Q. Will you have the kindness to put your initials upon it?

(The witness marked it J. B. S.)

Mr. Manager Butler (to the counsel for the respondent): The witness is yours, gentlemen.

Mr. Stanbery: Have you got through with this witness?

Mr. Manager Butler: I said the witness was yours, gentlemen.

Mr. Stanbery: Is that all you expect of this witness?

Mr. Manager Butler: All at present, and we may never recall him.

Cross examined by Mr. Evarts:

Q. You have produced a note-book of original stenographic report of a speech of the President? A. Yes, sir.

Q. Is it of the whole speech? A. Of the whole speech.

Q. Was it wholly made by you? A. By me; yes, sir.

Q. How long did the speech occupy in the delivery? A. Well, I suppose some twenty or twenty-five minutes.

JAMES O. CLEPHANE sworn and examined:

By Mr. Manager Butler:

Q. What is your business? A. I am at present deputy clerk of the Supreme Court of the District of Columbia.

Q. What was your employment on the 18th of August, 1866? A. I was then secretary to Governor Seward, Secretary of State.

Q. Are you a phonographic reporter? A. I am.

Q. How considerable has been your experience? A. Some eight or nine years.

Q. Were you employed on the 18th of August, 1866, to make a report of the President's speech in reply to Mr. Johnson? A. I was. I was engaged in connection with Mr. Smith for the Associated Press, and also for the *Daily Chronicle* at Washington.

Q. Did you make a report? A. I did.

Q. Where was this speech made? A. In the east room of the White House.

Q. You say it was in reply to Mr. Johnson? A. It was in reply to Hon. Reverdy Johnson.

Q. State partially who were present. A. There were a great many persons present—the committee of the convention. I noticed among the prominent personages General Grant, who stood beside the President during the

delivery of the speech.   Several reporters were present—
Mr. Murphy, Mr. Sheridan, Mr. Smith and others.

Q. Were any of the Cabinet officers present?   A. I do
not recollect whether any of them were present or not.

Q. Did you report that speech?   A. I did.

Q. What was done with that report? ·State all the circumstances.   A. With regard to the Associated Press report, I will state that Colonel Moore, the President's private secretary, desired the privilege of revising it before
publication; and, in order to expidite matters, Mr. Sheridan, Mr. Smith and myself united in the labor of
transcribing it; Mr. Sheridan transcribed one portion, Mr.
Smith another, and I a third.   After it was revised by
Colonel Moore, it was then taken and handed to the
agent of the Associated Press, who telegraphed it
throughout the country.

Q. Look at that roll of manuscript lying before you and
see if that is the speech that you transcribed and Moore
corrected.   A. (Having examined the manuscript produced by C. A. Tinker.)   I will state here that I do not
recognize any of my writing.   It is possible I may have
dictated to a long-hand writer on that occasion my portion, though I am not positive in regard to that.

Q. Who was present at the time of the writing out?
A. Mr. Smith, Mr. Sheridan and Colonel Moore, as far
as I recollect.

Q. Do you know Colonel Moore's handwriting?   A.
I do not.

LESSON XXXIV.

TRIAL OF ANDREW JOHNSON—*Continued.*

Q. Did you send your report to the *Chronicle?* A. I would state that Mr. McFarland, who had engaged me to report for the *Chronicle*, was unwilling to take the re-revised report of the President's speech as made by Colonel Moore. He desired to have the speech as it was delivered, as he stated, with all its imperfections, and, as he insisted upon my rewriting the speech, I did so, and it was published in the *Sunday Morning Chronicle* of the 19th.

Q. Have you a copy of that paper? A. I have not.

Q. After that report was published in the *Chronicle* of Sunday morning, the 19th, did you see the report? A. I did, sir, and examined it very carefully, because I had a little curiosity to see how it would read under the circumstances, being a literal report, with the exception of a word, perhaps, changed here and there.

Q. You say with the exception of a word changed here and there; how? A. Where the sentence was very awkward, and where the meaning was obscure, doubtless in that case I made a change. I recollect doing it in one or two instances, though I may not be able to point them out just now. If I had my original notes I could do so.

Q. With what certainty can you speak as to the *Chronicle's* report being an accurate one? A. I think I can speak with certainty as to its being accurate, a literal report, with the exception that I have named—perhaps a word or two here and there changed, in order to make the meaning more intelligible, or to make the sentence a little more round.

Cross examined by Mr. Evarts:

Q. You acted upon the employment of the Associated Press? A. Yes, sir; in connection with Mr. Smith.

Q. You were jointly to make a report, were you? A. We were to take the notes of the entire speech, each of us, and then we were to divide the labor of transcribing.

Q. Now, did you take phonographic notes of the whole speech? A. I did.

Q. Where are your phonographic notes? A. I have searched for them, but can not find them.

Q. Now, sir, at any time after you had completed the phonographic notes did you translate or write them out? A. I did.

.Q. The whole? A. The whole speech.

Q. Where is that translation or written transcript? A. I do not know, sir. The manuscript, of course, was left in the *Chronicle* office. I wrote it out for the *Chronicle*.

Q. You have never seen it since, have you? A. I have not.

Q. Have you made any search for it? A. I have not.

Q. And these two acts of yours, the phonographic report and the translation or writing out, are all that you had to do with the speech, are they? A. Yes, sir.

Q. Now, you say that subsequently you read a printed newspaper copy of the speech in the *Washington Chronicle?* A. Yes, sir.

Q. When was it that you read that newspaper copy? A. On the morning of the publication, August 19, Sunday morning.

Q. Where were you when you read it? A. I presume I was in my room; I generally saw the *Chronicle* there.

Q. And you there read it? A. Yes, sir.

Q. From this curiosity that you had? A. Yes; I read it more carefully because of that reason.

Q. Had you before you your phonographic notes, or your written transcript from them? A. I had not.

Q. And had not seen and never seen them in comparison before you? A. No, sir.

L. L. WALBRIDGE, sworn and examined:

By Mr. Manager Butler:

Q. What is your business? A. Short-hand writer.

Q. How long have you been engaged in that business? A. Nearly ten years.

Q. Have you had during that time any considerable experience; and if so, how much in that business? A. Yes, sir; I have had experience during the whole of that time in connection with newspaper reporting and outside.

(11)

Q. Reporting for courts?   A. Yes, sir.

Q. With what papers have you been lately connected?
A. More recently with the *Missouri Democrat;* previous
to that time with the *Missouri Republican.*

Q. Do the names of those papers indicate their party
proclivities, or are they reversed?   A. They are the reverse.

Q. The Democrat means Republican and the Republican means Democrat?   A. Exactly.

Q. To what paper were you attached on or about the
8th of September, 1866?   A. The *Missouri Democrat.*

Q. Did you report a speech delivered from the balcony
of the Southern Hotel in St. Louis by Andrew Johnson?
A. I did.

Q. What time in the day was that speech delivered?
A. Between eight and nine o'clock in the evening.

Q. Was there a crowd in the streets?   A. Yes, sir,
there was; and on the balcony also.

Q. Where were you?   A. I was on the balcony, within
two or three feet of the President while he was speaking.

Q. Where was the rest of the Presidential party?   A.
I can not tell you.

Q. Were they there?   A. I have no recollection of
seeing any of the party on the balcony.

·Q. Did the President come out to answer a call from
the crowd in the street apparently?   A. Yes, sir; I judge
so; I know there was a very large crowd in the street in
front of the hotel, and there were continuous cries for the
President, and in response to those cries I supposed he
came forward.

Q. Had he been received in the city by the procession of the various charitable societies? A. He had during the afternoon been received by the municipal authorities.

Q. Had the Mayor made him an address of welcome? A. He had.

Q. Had he answered the address? A. He had.

Q. Did you take a report of that speech? A. I did.

Q. How fully? A. I took every word.

Q. After it was taken, how soon was it written out? A. Immediately.

Q. How was it written out? A. At my dictation.

Q. By whom? A. The first part of the speech previous to the banquet was written out in one of the rooms of the Southern Hotel; that occupied about half an hour, I think; we then attended the banquet, at which other speeches were made. Immediately after the conclusion of the banquet we went to the *Republican* office and there I dictated the speech to Mr. Monahan and Mr. McHenry, two *attachés* of the *Republican*.

Q. You have spoken of a banquet; was there a banquet given to the President and his suite by the city? A. There was, at the Southern Hotel, immediately after the speech on the balcony.

Q. At that banquet did the President speak? A. He made a very short address.

Q. And there was other speaking there, I suppose? A. Yes, sir.

Q. After that speech was written out was it published? A. It was.

LESSON XXXV.

TRIAL OF ANDREW JOHNSON—*Continued.*

Q. When?   A. On the very next morning in the Sunday *Republican.*

Q. After it was published did you revise the publication by your notes?   A. I did.

Q. How soon?   A. Immediately after the speech was printed in the Sunday morning *Republican* I went to the *Democrat* office in company with my associate, Mr. Edmund T. Allen, and we very carefully revised the speech for the Monday morning *Democrat.*

Q. Then it was on the same Sunday that you made the revision?   A. Yes, sir; the Sunday after the speech.

Q. When you made the revision had you your notes? A. I had.

Q. State whether you compared the speech as printed with your notes?   A. Yes, sir; I did at that time, and since.

Q. When you compared it, did you make any corrections that were needed, if any were needed?   A. My recollection is that there were one or two simple corrections—errors either in transcribing or on the part of the printer; that is all I remember in the way of corrections of the speech.

Q. Did you afterward have occasion to revise that speech with your notes?   A. I had.

Q. When was that?   I think it was a little over a year ago.

Q. What occasion called you to revise it with your notes a little over a year ago?   A. I was summoned here by the Committee on the New Orleans Riot, and immediately after receiving the summons, I hunted up my notes and again made a comparison with them of the printed speech.

Q. How far did the second comparison assure you of corrections?   A. It was perfectly correct.

Q. Now, in regard to particularity of reporting; were you unable to report so correctly as to give inaccuracies of pronunciation?   A. Yes, sir; I did so in that instance.

Q. Where are your original notes now?   A. I can not tell you, sir; I searched for them immediately after I was summoned here, but failed to find them.

Q. You had them up to the time you were examined before the Committee on the New Orleans Riot?   A. I had, and brought them with me here, but I have no recollection of them since that time.

Q. Have you a copy of that paper?   A. I have.

Q. Will you produce it?   (The witness produces a newspaper, being the *Missouri Democrat* of Monday, September 10, 1866.)

Q. Is this it?   A. It is.

Q. From your knowledge of the manner in which you took the speech, and from your knowledge of the manner in which you corrected it, state whether you are now enabled to say that this paper which I hold in my hand contains an accurate report of the speech of the President delivered on that occasion? A. Yes, sir; I am enabled to say that it is an accurate report.

Mr. Manager Butler: I propose, if there is no objection, to offer this in evidence, and also if there is objection.

Mr. Evarts: Before that is done let us cross examine this witness.

Mr. Manager Butler: Certainly.

Cross examined by Mr. Evarts:

Q. I understand that you took down, as from the President's mouth, the entire speech, word for word as he delivered it? A. Yes, sir.

Q. In the transcript from your notes and in this publication, did you preserve that form and degree of accuracy and completeness? Is it all the speech? A. It is the whole speech.

Q. No part of it is condensed or paraphrased? A. No, sir; the whole speech is there in complete form.

Q. You say, that beside the revision of the speech which you made on the Sunday following its delivery, you made a revision a year ago? A. Yes, sir.

Q. For what reason and upon what occasion? A. As I said, it was owing to my having been summoned before the Committee on the New Orleans Riot.

Q. A Committee of Congress? A. Yes, sir.

Q. At Washington? A. Yes, sir.

Q. When was that? A. I should say a little over a year ago; I can not fix the date precisely.

Q. Were you then inquired of in regard to that speech? A. I was.

Q. And did you produce it then to that committee? A. I did.

Q. Were you examined before any other committee than that? A. No, sir.

Q. Was your testimony reduced to writing? A. I believe so.

Q. And signed by you? A. No, sir; not signed.

Mr. Evarts: We suppose, if the Court please, that this report is within the competency of proof.

Mr. Manager Butler (to the witness): Was your testimony published?

The Witness: The testimony I gave last winter?

Mr. Manager Butler: Yes, sir; before the New Orleans Riot Committee. A. I am not aware whether it was or not.

Mr. Manager Butler: Will the Secretary have the kindness to read this speech?

The Chief Clerk read as follows from the *Missouri Democrat* of Monday, September 10, 1866:

LESSON XXXVI.

LABOR TROUBLES IN PENNSYLVANIA.

INVESTIGATION BY THE HOUSE OF REPRESENTATIVES
—TO ACCOMPANY BILL H. R. 12,654, FEB-
RUARY 27, 1889.

TESTIMONY.

ISAAC A. SWEIGARD, sworn and examined.

By Mr. Parker:

Q. Where do you reside?   A. Philadelphia.

Q. What is your present employment?   A. General Superintendent of the Philadelphia & Reading Railroad.

Q. Where are you located?   A. 227 South Fourth Street.

Q. Is your business mainly located in the city or does it cover the whole road?   A. It covers the whole road.

Q. Does it include the Coal and Iron Company?   A. It does not.

Q. Simply the transportation of the road?   A. Yes, sir.

Q. How long have you been in this official position? A. About one year and three months.

Q. How long have you been engaged with the Reading Railroad?   A. Twenty-four years.

Q. State the capacities in which you have acted for it?
A. Clerk, agent, dispatcher, general dispatcher, division
superintendent, and general superintendent.

Q. Previous to becoming general superintendent what
were you? A. Division superintendent.

Q. You are familiar, then, with the lines of the road,
its points of business, its tracking, and its freight in its
whole extent? A. I am.

Q. Where were you at the time of the beginning of
the disturbances with the employees of your road last
year? A. At Philadelphia.

Q. State the first indications coming to you of such disturbances? A. About December, 1886.

Q. What were the indications? A. The men were
dissatisfied.

Q. Well what were the indications that they were dissatisfied? A. They were dissatisfied, in the first place,
with their wages and with their officers.

Q. What else? A. They complained of long hours.

Q. What else? A. They complained of not being received when they had a grievance.

Q. What else? A. That was about all.

Q. How did you know this? A. Well, they came —I
can not remember all of them.

Q. At different times? A. Yes, sir.

Q. Did they present any of these complaints in writing? A. Not at that time.

Q. State the date, as near as you can, when the first of

these complaints came to you? A. The latter part of November, I think.

Q. Do you remember the occasion? A. I do not.

Q. Do you not remember the particular occasion? A. I do not.

Q. You simply state they came to you? A. Yes.

Q. Upon what points were they complaining? A. Those that I mentioned.

Q. Wages, officers, long hours, and not being properly received; those were the complaints? A. Yes, sir.

Q. Did a committee call upon you? A. Yes, sir.

Q. A committee of whom? A. Knights of Labor.

Q. Do you remember the names of any of them? A. I do; some of them.

Q. State some of them? A. John Kelly, Joseph Cahill, Bennett, Sharkey.

Q. Did they present any writing at that time? A. They did.

Q. Have you a copy of it? A. I have not. I can not find it.

Q. What is the substance of it? A. It covered some fifteen or twenty points, I remember distinctly.

Q. What species of complaints, if any, were covered additional to the four you have stated? A. There were about four species, but put in different form.

Q. About how long was this document? A. I suppose it was eighteen inches.

Q. Well, about how many words? A. I do not know that.

Q. How many pages of writing? A. About two pages of foolscap, I should judge.

Q. In writing? A. Yes, in writing.

Q. What did you do with that paper? A. The committee and I had that paper for two days in my office.

Q. Who had it? A. The committee and myself had it.

Q. This same committee? A. Yes, sir. I took two days to go over the matter. I found they had some grievances, and, knowing the men for years, I thought it was proper they should be met, and I did meet them, and we adjusted the difficulties there and then; the latter part of December or the first of January—I think about the 24th or 25th of December, 1886. I tried to find that paper this morning and yesterday, but I have not been able to find it.

Q. Well, as the result, was there a full agreement upon the point presented, and an adjustment that you understood to be satisfactory to both parties? A. Yes, sir; there was.

Q. When was the next disturbance occurring between the railroad employees and the railroad officers? A. We had no disturbance after that agreement; we got along very nicely together for three or four months.

Q. Was there any written agreement as the result of this negotiation? A. There was; they have got a copy of that.

Q. Has the company a copy? A. I think it has.

Q. Have you a copy of it? A. I think so; I have not it

with me, but the committee has.   It is filed in Assembly
6285, Port Richmond.

Q. Will you present that copy?   A. I will if I can find
it.   You can get it from them if they have it.   It is
signed by myself.

Q. But sometimes there is difficulty in getting docu-
ments from societies, but we do not expect any trouble
from the railroad, of course, and if you will produce it, you
will oblige us.   Now, if you will go on to the next disturbance?   A. Possibly three or four months; I can not fix
the time.

Q. Do it as near as you can, and tell us what occurred
then?   A. Well, at different points the men became dissatisfied.   For instance, we would make a promotion; we
might promote a certain man to the position of dispatcher,
and the men would object to it; or possibly we would
order engines from one division to another to do some
certain work, and as soon as the engine reached that point
the men would stop work, which was positively against
the agreement.   Our agreement was, that in case any
trouble might arise, a committee should see me, and that
no man should stop work until after this committee had
called upon me; but they failed to do that.

Q. Was that a part of the written agreement to which
you have referred?   A. That was a part of it.

Q. Will you give us the date of that agreement?   A.
I can not.

Q. Well, about when?   A. I think it was about the
24th or 25th of December.

Q. Was not the agreement dated later? A. I do not want to tell you anything I do not know. I am trying to tell you the truth.

Q. The 24th or 25th of December? A. Yes, as near as I can say; it might have been in January. If it was January, it was 1887. If that agreement is not the 24th or 25th of December, 1886, it is January, 1887.

ECKLEY B. COXE, sworn and examined.

By Mr. Stone:

Q. Where do you live? A. Drifton, Luzerne County, Pa.

Q. How long have you lived in that vicinity? A. I have been a resident of the village since 1865, but I have lived off and on in the neighborhood ever since I was six weeks old. In fact the ground on which I live has belonged to my father and grandfather for nearly a hundred years. Since I grew up I have lived mostly at Drifton. When I went there it was a wilderness.

Q. Do you hold any official position in Pennsylvania? A. I have no official position whatever.

Q. I thought you were State Senator? A. I was elected in 1880, but my term expired at the end of 1884. I represented, at that time, the district in which I now live.

Q. What business are you engaged in? A. I am a mining engineer by profession and am engaged in the mining of coal.

Q. The mining of anthracite coal in that region? A. In what is known as the Lehigh region.

LESSON XXXVII.

LABOR TROUBLES IN PENNSYLVANIA—*Continued.*

Q. How long have you been engaged in that business?
A. Since February 5, 1865, as a coal operator. Previous
to that I was interested in the management of the estate
of my grandfather.

Q. How many men had you in your employ in September, 1887, engaged in the mining of coal? A. It is
necessary, perhaps, to explain the division of the employees. After the coal comes from the mine, a very large
amount of work has to be done to prepare it for market,
hence there are two classes of workmen, those working
under ground and those engaged in the preparation of the
coal for market, such as sorting, crushing, and taking
slate out of the coal. This is done outside. Then we
have a large number of men that are to be employed as
teamsters, outside laborers, carpenters, etc. Our employees
in the month of August—they were paid for August in
September, just at the beginning of the strike—there
were in the mining department, 1,840; preparation department, 1,279; outside department, by which we mean
teamsters, laborers, and men not doing work in the breakers nor under ground, 366; machinery department, 155;
construction department, 6; miscellaneous, 53. Miscellaneous includes clerks and men of that kind, making a

total of 3,699. In the selling department we have 193. These have charge of the selling of the coal.

Q. How many men had you in your employ connected with the mining of coal in December, 1887? A. In the mining department, 469, instead of 1,840; in the preparation department, 389, instead of 1,279; in the outside department, 95, instead of 366; in the machinery department, 128, instead of 155; in the construction department, 3, instead of 6; and miscellaneous, 50, instead of 53; and in the selling department, 140, instead of 193.

Q. Can you state how many men you now have in your employ compared with the number you had in December? A. In December we had about 30 per cent., and now I suppose about 35 per cent. to 37 per cent. of what we had in August. We have more than we had in December, probably 5 per cent. more.

Q. You have classified these employees, and among others you have a mining department? A. That includes all men who are engaged either in cutting coal, loading coal, and transporting coal under ground; that is, drivers, locomotive engineers, etc., and those engaged in keeping up the timber, roads, etc. It includes everybody who works under ground except the men engaged about the pumps and machinery.

Q. Now the preparation department embraces what? A. It embraces all men we consider belonging to the business of mining that work on the surface, except the machinery department. That department is kept entirely separate. That is a special kind of labor requiring mechanics and workmen of that kind.

Q. You have a class denominated outside department? A. This comprises the teamsters and stable-men, workmen engaged in keeping up roads and digging cellars, ditches, and things of that kind, etc. There is a great deal of work not belonging to mining; for example, if a man living in one of our houses comes in and says his cellar is full of water, we have to send men to attend to it. It also includes men that cut timber and work in the sawmills, of which there are a large number.

Q. What do you mean by construction department? A. That department comprises those engaged in the building of houses, breakers, or any building. Sometimes it runs down practically to nothing, but if we were building a large number of houses, we might have 40 or 50 or 100 men in this department. They are mechanics who work sometimes for us and sometimes for others. If we were building a large number of houses, we would give notice that we wanted so many carpenters, and we might hire 50 to 100.

Q. Do you hire by contract? A. We hire them by the day. They are men who do not work the year round for us.

Q. Now the miscellaneous department? A. It consists principally of men who perform clerical work, odds and ends, watchmen, etc. In about four or five thousand men there are a lot of men it is difficult to classify.

Q. Under what head are police classified? A. They

are not our employees. If they were our employees they would be under the outside department. The police are paid by the operators, I believe. I think there are one or two operators who do not contribute. There is a secretary, I know, and he sends us a bill each month for our share, dependent upon the amount of service we require.

Q. Now the selling department? A. That includes our employees in New York, Boston, Milwaukee, Chicago, Buffalo and Philadelphia. They are men who sell the coal, and includes also the men who work on our boats and docks, where we ship. The tide coal is sent to Port Johnson, South Amboy and Perth Amboy, and there it is dumped from the cars through chutes into boats; and the same is true at Buffalo.

Q. Into your boats? A. We have boats of our own in New York, but in the West large vessels are used which we have no interest in.

Q. Do you have the men managing your boats classified under this head? A. They are in the selling department. It is entirely separate from the mining business.

Q. How many sales agents have you? A. We have one general sales agent. He has an assistant in New York, one in Boston, one in Chicago and one in Philadelphia. He has general charge.

Q. Have you a sales agent at Philadelphia? A. yes; Mr. Eldridge.

(12)

LESSON XXXVIII.

THE ALLEGED ELECTION OUTRAGES IN TEXAS.

REPORTED BY THE COMMITTEE ON PRIVILEGES AND ELECTIONS OF THE UNITED STATES SENATE.

WASHINGTON, D. C., February 22, 1887.

The sub-committee met pursuant to adjournment at 10:30 o'clock A. M.

TESTIMONY.

LAFAYETTE KIRK, having been duly sworn, was interrogated as follows:

By Mr. Spooner:

Q. What is your name?   A. Lafayette Kirk.

Q. Where do you reside?   A. In Brenham, Washington County, Texas.

Q. How long have you lived there?   A. I have lived in Brenham since September, 1880.

Q. What is your business?   A. I am a lawyer by profession.

Q. What are you by practice?   A. I am a lawyer.

Q. Then you are a practicing lawyer?   A. Yes, sir.

Q. How long have you been engaged in practicing law? A. I was admitted to the bar in the spring of 1881; I commenced practice in the fall of 1881.

Q. Do you hold any official position in Washington County? A. Yes, sir; I am county judge of Washington County.

Q. How long have you been county judge of Washington County? A. Since November, 1884.

Q. What is the jurisdiction of your court? What I want to get at is the principal functions which you discharge as county judge? A. The County Court has original jurisdiction of all controversies where the amount exceeds $200 and does not exceed $500; it has concurrent jurisdiction with the District Court where the amount exceeds $500 and does not exceed $1000; it has jurisdiction for final disposition of all criminal cases where the penalty involves a fine or imprisonment in the county jail.

Q. It has original jurisdiction to punish? A. Yes, sir; and it has final jurisdiction of that class of cases.

Q. Do you mean that there is no appeal? A. There is an appeal, but it finally disposes of the cases.

Q. What functions do you discharge in connection with the canvass of the vote? A. I preside over all meetings of the Commissioners' Court, and one of the duties of the Commissioners' Court is to canvass the return of the vote, and when that is done, it is the duty of the county judge, as such presiding officer, to issue certificates of election to parties who are declared elected as the result of the count.

Q. When did you first learn of the decision of the Supreme Court of the State of Texas as to the legality of the diamond-shaped tickets? A. I never read it until it was read here the other day.

Q. That is not an answer to my question. A. I heard it discussed immediately after the late election in Washington County in 1886, when there was some talk of the contesting of the election.

Q. It had been for some months published, had it not, in your Texas Supreme Court reports? A. Yes, sir; it had been published some time before the election.

Q. How long before the election? A. I do not know; ten or twelve months, I presume.

Q. You are furnished by the state with a copy of the Supreme Court reports? A. Yes, sir; I have a copy of the reports.

By Mr. Eustis:

Q. If it was rendered in 1885, it could not have been twelve months before? A. I do not know how long it was before.

By Mr. Spooner:

Q. You are furnished by the state with these reports? A. Yes, sir.

Q. Do you wish it to be understood that you do not read the reports and familiarize yourself with the decisions of your State Court? A. I wish to be understood that I never had any occasion to investigate the election law.

Q. It is a part of your business to preside at the canvassing of the election returns? Yes, sir.

Q. And yet you did not consider it a matter of any interest to look up the decisions of your Supreme Court in regard to the election laws? A. I had no right under the election laws to go into the polling places and see what was done in there.

Q. I repeat the question: You did not consider it a matter of any interest to look up the decision of your Supreme Court in regard to the election laws? A. No, sir; I had studied the law before, and I was governed by that, and had no special occasion to read that decision.

Q. I did not ask you if you had any special reason to investigate it. A. Well, I never had read it; I will state, in that connection, what my duties were in canvassing the votes.

Q. You may state it. A. The presiding judges of the election at the different precincts make out a return, and in that return they indicate how many votes each candidate received, and I am governed entirely by that.

Q. Are not the ballots returned? A. The ballots are counted and thrown in a box.

Q. Are not the original ballots returned in order that the county canvassers may decide whether they are to be counted or not? A. They are not returned for that purpose; they are returned, as was done in this case, in order that if there should be a contest they could be there and could be opened by the district judge; that is the only court which has authority or right to try contested-election cases, and the only legal authority to open any election-box at all or to examine any ticket.

Q. All the canvassing you do then is to canvass the vote as returned? A. Yes; as returned by the presiding justices of the different precincts of the election, who make no decision as to the legality or illegality of any vote cast at all; they are governed completely by the return of the presiding officer.

Q. Do you know whether the diamond-shaped tickets cast in any of the Democratic precincts were counted, and the Republican diamond-shaped tickets cast at Independence were cast out? A. I do not know about that other than from hearsay.

Q. Were there any lawyers on that board except yourself? A. I am the only lawyer on the Commissioners' Court; I am the only member of the board who is a lawyer.

Q. Did you give any advice on election day as to the validity of these diamond-shaped tickets? A. I did not.

Q. How long had you been county judge? A. I had been county judge for two years.

Q. How long had you known Dewees Boulton? A. I had known him for a number of years.

Q. Intimately? A. Not very intimately; he lived at a remote part of the county, and I would see him occasionally, perhaps two or three times a year.

Q. What was he in politics? A. He was a Democrat.

Q. Was he active in politics? A. No, sir; he was not active at all.

Q. He was pretty active in the campaign of 1886, was he not? A. He was not active in the campaign of 1886.

Q. By active you mean that he did not make speeches? A. He did not make speeches or attend meetings.

LESSON XXXIX.

ALLEGED ELECTION OUTRAGES IN TEXAS—*Continued.*

Q. Didn't he go with you to any meetings? A. No, sir; he never went with me to a meeting during any canvass.

Q. Did you have any consultation with him in regard to election right before election? A. I did not.

Q. Were you with him in Brenham the day before election? A. I met him in Searcy & Bryan's office; he came there to get the election tickets to take to the polls; I exchanged no words with him except a greeting.

Q. He came there the day before election to get the election tickets? Yes, sir; and took them out there.

Q. Well, he came there to get them? A. Yes, sir.

Q. And got them? A. Yes, sir; he got them.

Q. And you met him? A. Yes, sir; I met him.

Q. But you had no talk with him? A. I had no conversation with him except to say how do you do; that is, perhaps, about all.

Q. You say that is about all; is it all? A. It is all that I remember.

Q. Didn't you have considerable conversation with him that day as to what should be done the next day in the negro precincts? A. I had no conversation with him whatever as to what should be done there the next day.

Q. Where were you on election day? A. I was in Brenham the most of the day.

Q. What part of the day were you there? A. I was there until 4 or 5 o'clock, I presume; I can not remember definitely the time I left Brenham.

Q. You did leave Brenham? A. I did leave Brenham; yes, sir.

Q. Did you leave Brenham before the polls closed? A. Yes, sir.

Q. How long before the polls closed? A. I suppose it was about an hour or an hour and a half.

Q. What report had you up to that time from the Washington precinct as to how it was going? A. I had no definite report at all.

Q. I did not ask you that. A. Well, I had heard, I think, some one had received a telegram there stating that it was mixed.

Q. Who had received that telegram? A. I do not remember who had received it; I did not see the telegram.

Q. Is it not true that a report was received and that you heard it, that that precinct was giving an unusually large Republican majority? A. It is not; it is not true; I did not hear any such report.

Q. What time did you leave Brenham, if you did leave there? A. I left there, I think, about 5 o'clock in the afternoon.

Q. How did you go away? A. I went on horseback.

Q. Where did you go to? A. To Chapel Hill.

Q. How far was that from Brenham? A. About ten miles.

Q. Where did you go from Chapel Hill? A. To Flewellen voting place.

Q. How far was that from Brenham? A. I suppose about fourteen or fifteen miles.

HENRY MULLER, having been duly sworn, was interrogated as follows:

By Mr. Eustis:

Q. What is your full name? A. Henry Muller.

Q. How old are you? A. I am forty-four years old.

Q. Where do you live? A. At Brenham, Texas.

Q. How long have you lived there? A. At Brenham about fourteen years.

Q. What is your business? A. I am publishing a newspaper and keeping a book-store.

Q. What is the name of the paper? A. The Texas *Volksbote.*

Q. What are your politics? A. I am a Republican.

Q. How long have you been a Republican? A. About twenty-seven years.

Q. Are you a Republican now? A. I am.

Q. Were you in the army during the war? A. I was.

Q. On which side? A. On the Union side.

Q. Are you drawing your pension now? A. I am.

Q. Were you an officer or a private soldier? A. A private soldier.

Q. How long were you in the army? A. I was in the

army from the beginning until the close of the war, and a little after. I served five years in the volunteer service, and after that I served in the regular army.

Q. Who did you support in the last Presidential election? A. Mr. Blaine.

Q. Did you vote for him? A. I voted for him, and worked for him.

Q. Did your paper advocate his election? A. Yes, sir; strongly.

Q. What ticket did you support at the last election in November, 1886? A. I supported the People's ticket in Washington County.

Q. What ticket did you support in 1884—the local ticket, I mean? A. In 1884 I didn't take any strong stand as to county elections. I advised the people to vote for the best men. I supported the Republican ticket in 1884; I mean in state and national affairs.

Q. What local ticket did your paper support in 1886—the last election? A. What is called the People's ticket.

Q. How was that ticket formed, and what was the occasion of forming it? A. That ticket in 1886 was simply formed by a petition signed by hundreds of citizens of both parties requesting the then present officers to run again for their respective offices—the county offices.

Q. Can you state about how many signed that call? A. It must have been something like 800, possibly 900; I do not know exactly.

Q. From your knowledge of the people there do you remember whether it was signed irrespective of party, so far as national politics were concerned? A. It was irrespecive of party so far as I know. It had the names of a great many Republicans on it also, and colored men, colored Republicans.

Q. Why is it that the Republicans, white and colored, supported the People's ticket in 1884 and 1886? A. In 1884 I must say that I was not present at Brenham when the People's ticket was nominated, but being a newspaper man I had occasion to inquire into causes. It was formed because the citizens were dissatisfied with the mode the county administration was conducted, and they resolved to put in good men for office and elect them irrespective of politics.

Q. Do I understand you to mean that respectable Republicans were dissatisfied with the local Republican administration of affairs? A. Yes, sir.

Q. Do you mean men, for instance, who were property holders? A. Yes, sir; property holders.

Q. And people interested in good government? A. Yes, sir.

Mr. Evarts: He does not say all of them.

The witness: No, sir; I did not say all of them.

Q. I suppose you know quite a number of respectable Republicans in Brenham? A. Yes, sir.

Q. Is any man, from the mere fact that he is a Republican, at all molested in that community? A. No, sir.

Q. Either in his social relations or his business relations or any other relations? A. Not on account of his politics; I have never known an act of that kind.

LESSON XL.

ALLEGED ELECTION OUTRAGES IN TEXAS—*Continued.*

Q. How long has that been so?   A. That has been so ever since I have been in Texas, where I live.

Q. So that a Republican who attends to his business and works and votes for his party, who himself is a man of good standing and not obnoxious to the community, I understand you to say, is on precisely the same footing as a Democratic citizen would be?   A. Yes, sir ; he has the same rights and is not molested.

Q. And there is no distinction made against him?   A. No, sir.

Q. So far as your observation extends, are not the people in that community a law-abiding, peaceable people? A. Yes, sir; they are.

Q. People who want good government?   A. Yes, sir; they are that.

Q. Is not one of the causes of prejudice against these gentlemen you have mentioned their attempt to control and unite the negro people and the negro vote against the white people and the white vote?   A. That is understood so.

Q. Is not that very dangerous to the peace of the community?   A. It is at times.

Q. And that is deprecated, is it not, by the good people of that community, Democrats and Republicans?   A. I would say that the uniting of the colored vote is not so much deprecated as the uniting of the colored vote to support men whom the people do not respect or like.

By Mr. Evarts:

Q. Do you think the hanging of the three men who were taken from the jail was an indication of a law-abiding spirit down there? A. I do not.

Q. Do you think the disposition and conduct of the community there after this last election in raiding the ballot-boxes and breaking up the election and defeating it, indicated a law-abiding people? A. I do not.

Q. What instances can you name indicating this to be a law-abiding community. What instances can you mention as having occurred between the 2d of November and the 4th of December last? A. The quiet and orderly condition of our city of Brenham, I can instance as one. That is the place where I live, and that place is the only one I can mention, as I have been nowhere else.

Q. Between the 2d of November and the 4th of December last? A. Yes, sir.

Q. The quiet of that town? A. Yes, sir.

Q. Can you name any other indication of a law-abiding people? A. The indication of a law-abiding people may perhaps be found in the circumstances that nothing occurred to disturb the law except the hanging of those negroes.

Q. That is, that there was no more hanging than that? A. Yes; hanging or violence of any kind.

Q. You think that indicates a law-abiding people; that there were no more hangings or violence? - A. I do not think that; I only said that I could not name anything specially, and that nothing occurred in violation of the laws except that.

Q. You did not observe any movement in that community towards disapproving of violence at the ballot-boxes, or disapproving of the hanging, did you? A. That has been expressed by citizens of all parties; a disapproval of that hanging; I have done that in my paper, and it has been also expressed at the public meeting at Burton that I read of.

Q. That was not at Brenham then? A. No, sir.

Q. Well, let us have Brenham; that is where you live; go on with your indications of a law-abiding community between the 2d of November and the 4th of December. A. Very well; some time after the election the meeting of citizens was held at Brenham—

Q. Do you mean the meeting at Eldredge Hall? A. Yes, sir; the one at Eldredge Hall.

Q. Do you give that as an indication of a law-abiding people? A. I give that as one.

Q. Very well; give us now any other. A. I do not know but there were two meetings held there, at which it was resolved to keep up peace and order.

Q. You have given us one meeting; we know what took place there. Now, name any other meeting which you think shows an indication of a law-abiding people. A. There are none that I can remember now.

Q. You say that individuals expressed opinions adverse to violence and disturbance? A. Yes, sir.

Q. And that you also did in your newspaper? A. Yes, sir.

Q. Did you ever hear of the Democratic party or the Democratic citizens there uniting in any movement to show that they disapproved of raiding the ballot-boxes or of hanging these men; I mean there at your place of Brenham? A. I think that was expressed in the meeting held about two or three weeks ago, in which all this violence was deprecated.

Q. That is, you mean a meeting held two or three weeks ago from the present time? A. Yes, sir; two or three weeks ago.

Q. Since the Senate commenced this investigation? A. I think so.

Q. But up to that time you had not heard of any movement of the kind in that community, had you?

The Witness: After which time?

Mr. Evarts: Up to this meeting held three weeks ago. You have named a meeting which took place two or three weeks ago that showed a loyalty to law, and so forth? A. Yes, sir.

Q. But up to that time, had there been any movement? A. I think the same had been expressed in the meeting at Eldredge Hall.

Q. But, except in that one case? A. Except that, I do not know of any other.

JAMES E. SLATER, having been duly sworn, was interrogated as follows:

By Senator Spooner:

Q. You have been examined before in this investigation, have you not?   A. Yes, sir.

Q. You reside at Brenham?   A. Yes, sir.

Q. You are telegraph operator at Brenham?   A. Yes, sir; at Brenham, Texas.

Q. How long have you been operator at that place?   A. The last time since 1880, but I was in the office before.

Q. Were you in charge of the office there in 1886?   A. Yes, sir.

Q. Have you ever seen this before (showing a telegram to the witness)?   A. I of course have seen it because the words " seven, paid," are in my handwriting, and " filed 12 M," is in my handwriting, and the time of the message sent to Houston is in my handwriting.

Q. What time was it sent to Houston?   A. It was sent to Houston at 12.50 P. M., it says here.

Q. That was received by you to be transmitted at 12 M. on November 2, 1886?   A. Yes, sir.

Q. And was transmitted by you?   A. Yes, sir; there is the evidence of it.

Q. It was transmitted at 12.50 P. M.?   A. This is the evidence of it.

Q. That is the memorandum made by you at that time?   A. Yes, sir ; at the time.   We mark the messages as we send them.   When we receive a message we put in here (indicating) when they were filed. It was received at 12 o'clock to send to Houston.

Q. This is the original of the message which was handed to you for transmission? A. Yes, sir.

Q. And you sent it to Courtney by way of Houston? A. Yes, sir.

Q. Do you know the handwriting in which it is? A. No, sir.

(13)

LESSON XLI.

COURT PROCEEDINGS.

SUPREME COURT OF OHIO.

I. J. MILLER AND GUSTAV TAFEL,
TRUSTEES,

vs.

WILLIAM HENRY ELDER, *et al.*

JOHN B. MANNIX, ASSIGNEE,
                    Plaintiff in Error,

vs.

WILLIAM HENRY ELDER, *et al.,*
                    Defendants in Error.

DEPOSITIONS.

JOHN B. PURCELL, sworn, deposes as follows:

Q. State your name, age, residence and occupation, or office?   A. John B. Purcell, age 81, Cincinnati, Bishop of the Roman Catholic Diocese of Cincinnati.

Q. Please state how long you have held the office of Bishop.   A. Since 1833.

Q. Please state by whom you were appointed?   A. By Gregory XVI, Pope of Rome.

Q. Please state what office in said church you held prior to your appointment as such Bishop, and for what length of time. A. I was professor and president of the College of Mt. St. Mary's, Emmittsburg, Maryland. I can hardly tell the length of time. I went when professor to Paris and was there four years.

Q. Please state who was your predecessor as Archbishop. A. Bishop Edward Fenwick was my predecessor.

Q. At the time of your appointment as Bishop of the diocese of Cincinnati, please state what territory or counties were embraced in such diocese. A. The State of Ohio, and subsequently the towns of Newport and Covington, Ky., for a time.

Q. State whether or not such territory has since been reduced by the creation of new dioceses or otherwise; if so, at what time and to what extent. A. The territory was decreased by the creation of a new diocese in Cleveland and a new diocese in Covington, Ky.; I can hardly state at what time; also, Columbus, Ohio.

Q. Please state in whom was vested the title to the real estate in such diocese of Cincinnati, devoted to the ecclesiastical or educational purposes of said church, at the time of the assignment mentioned in the petition, viz.: in the month of March, 1879.

Question objected to.

A. In the name of John B. Purcell.

Q. State by what authority the title to said property was vested in you. A. By the authority of the Catholic

Church and the consent of all the people in my capacity as Bishop of the diocese.

Q. Please state what, if any, limitation was or is placed upon your control or right to dispose of such property by said authority, or by the laws of said church.   A. None.

Q. Please state in general terms the extent of your authority over such property under the rules or laws of said church.   A. To make a right and just use of it for the interest of the church.

Q. Please state what is the general law of said church regulating the acquisition, control and disposition by its bishops of real estate held for religious, educational or other purposes.   A. That they faithfully administer it for the purpose for which it came into their hands.

Q. Please state what, if any, authority under the laws and rules of the Catholic Church have congregations of said church to dispose, or direct, or restrain the disposition by you of any property, occupied by them, but held in your name by virtue of your office of Archbishop. A. None without my consent, which, I might add, is always granted when deemed expedient and proper.

Q. Please state whether or not the congregations exercise the right of disposition without your consent, or does such disposition by them rest entirely in your discretion? A. As I said before, whenever it is deemed expedient the disposition is granted; not without it.

Q. Please state, then, who is to judge of the expediency.   A. The Bishop consulting with the people— in council with the people; trustees we have none.

Q. Please state what, if any, limit is there to the free exercise of your discretion of your judgment in determining the necessity of expediency of the alienation or disposition of the property so held in your name. A. By an appeal of the people of the congregation to Rome, which can limit and set aside my authority.

Q. Please state whether or not that is the only limit to your authority. A. Of course it is understood as to my authority over such property; it is the only limit.

Q. State whether or not you mean to say by the last answer that the only limit to the free exercise of your discretion as to the alienation or disposition of .said property is the right to appeal to Rome? A. That is the only one I know of.

Q. Please state who, if any one other than yourself, has attended to the financial affairs of your diocese during your episcopacy. A. My brother, Rev. Edward Purcell.

Q. By what authority, verbal or written? A. By both.

Q. Please state how long since he commenced attending to said financial affairs. A. I can not exactly say; since he became a priest, since he has been admitted to the priesthood, in 1838.

Q. Please state to the extent of the authority given by you to him as such agent. A. It was the same I had myself, to manage temporal matters in my name and for my benefit and the benefit of the church.

Q. Please state whether or not you authorized any other agent or agents to act for you during that time in matters of business or finance. A. I did not that I remember.

LESSON XLII.

COURT PROCEEDINGS—*Continued.*

Q. State what was the nature of the business transacted by Edward Purcell as your agent. A. It was for the purchase of property, for churches, and schools and asylums.

Q. Please state whether or not it was in the course of business as your agent that Edward Purcell received moneys on deposit and gave his notes or receipt therefor. A. It was.

Q. Please state for what purpose such deposits were received by him as your agent. A. To pay for lots, churches and schools for charities, orphan asylums, houses of refuge.

Q. Please state when the ground was bought on which the cathedral is built, and when the buildings were erected. A. As well as I can remember it was bought some time in 1830. I can't say exactly the year. It was bought from Judge Burnet; the buildings were in progress of erection for eight years ; in 1844 the church was dedicated; from 1838 to 1844 they were built.

Q. Please state what income, if any; you had at the time of the purchase of said ground and the erection of said buildings. A. My only income was what I expected from the charity of the people; from charity; I had no income.

Q. Please state if you know the cost of said property and improvements. A. The cathedral lot cost $24,000, the cathedral, the shell of the building, cost $120,000.

Q. Who paid for the ground and the improvements? A. Charity.

Q. Who received and disbursed such charity? A. Chiefly, if not exclusively, my brother.

Q. Please state what portion of the cost of said ground and improvements was donated to you, or him for you, in the form of charity. A. I can hardly answer; I might say all that still remains unpaid.

Q. Please state, if you can, what was the cause of your brother, Edward Purcell, receiving money on deposit at interest. A. It was to pay for lots and buildings and the expenses incident thereto, taxes and the like.

Q. Please state as nearly as you can what portion of said $60,000 was received by you prior to the purchase of the cathedral lot, or during the erection of the buildings thereon, and how much, if any, has been received since that time. A. None for the purpose of the buildings here, or before the purchase of the cathedral lot and the commencement and erection of the buildings.

Q. State if you know, then, what portion of said sum. was applied to payment of the cathedral grounds and building. A. I don't know how much, because I was always engaged in other buildings and purchases besides the cathedral.

Q. Please state during what period of time it was that you received said $60,000 by way of charitable contributions and donations.   A. It was since I became Bishop that I received this sum, up to the present time; since I became Bishop in 1833.

Q. When did you obtain the title to the ground on which the seminary is built, and from whom and for what consideration? A. I received it from the Considine family; they gave me the ground gratis.

Q. Who erected the seminary?   A. John and James Slevin mainly, and my brother, Edward Purcell.   I believe Mrs. Corr gave about $5,000 or $10,000, and $5,000 at two different times.   Mr. Boyle gave, I think, $5,000.

Q. Please state, if you know, the amount of money that your brother, Edward Purcell, expended in erecting the buildings on the seminary grounds, and whether or not such money so expended by him came in whole or in part from moneys received by him on deposit, and for which he had given his individual obligation.

Form of the question objected to.

A. I do not know how much he expended or how much he got from deposits.   I left those things to him.

Q. State whether or not any record was kept by you of sums contributed in charity and used in the purchase of .the cathedral lot, the erection of buildings thereon and the erection of the seminary.   A. I have no record but what I have stated.   Mr. Slevin spent $22,000.

Q. Please state whether or not all charitable contributions passed through the hands of Edward Purcell. A. As far as I know they did.

.Q. Please state where students for the priesthood were

educated and at whose expense before the building of Mt. St. Mary's Seminary. A. I will say at various places, Paris particularly. Paris, France; at St. Martins, Brown County, Ohio, and at my expense ; and in addition at the Barons Mission and at the American College at Rome.

Q. Please state by whom the Orphan Asylum ground in Cumminsville was purchased, and where the purchase money came from. A. They were purchased by me, and the money came from borrowed money or charity.

LESSON XLIII.

ARTICLES OF COPARTNERSHIP.

Articles of copartnership made this 5th day of June, 1890, by and between Edward Dawson and Henry A. Perkins, both of the City of Albany.

The said parties hereby agree to form and do form a copartnership for the purpose of carrying on the general produce and commission business on the following terms and articles of agreement, to the faithful performance of which they mutually engage and bind themselves.

The style and name of the copartnership shall be Dawson & Perkins, and shall commence on the 1st day of July, 1890.

Each of said parties agrees to contribute to the funds of the partnership the sum of $1,000 in cash, which shall be paid in on or before the 1st day of July, 1890, and each of said parties shall devote and give all his time and attention to the business, and to the care and superintendence of the same.

All profits which may accrue to the said partnership shall be divided, and all losses happening to the said firm, whether from bad debts, depreciation of goods, or any other cause or accident, and all expenses of the business shall be borne by the said parties equally.

All the purchases, sales, transactions and accounts of the said firm shall be kept in regular books, which shall be always open to the inspection of both parties and their legal representatives, respectively. An account of stock shall be taken, and an account between the parties shall be settled as often as once a year, and as much oftener as either partner may desire and in writing request.

Neither of the said parties shall subscribe any bond, sign or indorse any note of hand, accept, sign or indorse any draft or bill of exchange, or assume any other liability, verbal or written, either in his own name or the name of the firm, for the accommodation of any other person or persons whatsoever, without the consent in writing of the other party; nor shall either party lend any of the funds of the copartnership without such consent of the other party.

Neither party shall be engaged in any other business, nor shall either party withdraw from the joint stock any more than $91 per quarter, or $364 per year.

On the dissolution of this copartnership, if the said parties, or their legal representatives, can not agree in the division of the stock then on hand, the whole copartnership effects, except the debts due the firm, shall be sold at public auction, at which both parties shall be at liberty to bid and purchase like other individuals, and the proceeds to be divided after paying the debts of the firm.

For the purpose of securing the performance of the foregoing agreements it is agreed that either party, in case of any violation of them, or either of them, by the other, shall have the right to dissolve this copartnership forthwith on his becoming informed of such violation.

In witness whereof the said parties have hereto set their hands and seals the day and year first above written.

EDWARD DAWSON,　　[L. S.]

HENRY A. PERKINS,·　[L. S.]

CERTIFICATE OF ORGANIZATION OF A BANKING 'ASSOCIATION.

To all to whom these presents shall come, greeting :

We, whose hands and seals are hereunto subscribed, having associated ourselves under and pursuant to the act of the Legislature of the State of New York, entitled, "An Act to Authorize the Business of Banking," and the several acts amendatory thereof, to establish an office of discount, deposit and circulation, and carry on the business of banking, do hereby certify:

1.　That the name assumed to distinguish such association and to be used in its dealings is, "The Merchants' National Bank."

2.　The operations of discount and deposit of such association are to be carried on in the city of Troy, in the County of Rensselaer, in the State of New York.

3. ·　The amount of the capital stock of such association is $300,000, and the same is divided into three thousand shares of $100 each (and in the articles of association provision is made authorizing an increase of such capital, and of the number of associates from time to time, as may be

deemed proper, to an amount not exceeding $500,000 in the aggregate).

4.   The names and places of residence of the share-holders and the number of shares held by each of them respectively, fully appear by the signatures and subscriptions hereto.   .

5.   The period at which such association shall commence is the 10th day of March, 1858, and the period at which the same shall terminate is the 10th day of March, 1898.

In testimony whereof we have on the 10th day of January, in the year 1858, hereto respectively subscribed our hands and seals, and specified our respective places of residence, and the number of shares of the capital stock of the association aforesaid taken and held by each of us respectively.

| Name. | Residence. | Number of Shares. |

LESSON XLIV.

LEASE.

A lease made and executed between George L. Williams, of the City of Rochester, State of New York, of the first part, and James D. Randall, of the City of Toledo, State of Ohio, of the second part, the first day of July, in the year of our Lord one thousand, eight hundred and seventy-one.

In consideration of the rents and covenants hereinafter expressed, the said party of the first part has demised and leased, and does hereby demise and lease to the said party of the second part, the following premises, viz.:

The two-story brick dwelling house known as No. 10 Elizabeth Street, in the City of Rochester aforesaid, with the privileges and appurtenances, for and during the term of three years and nine months from the date hereof, which term will end April 1, 1875. And the said party of the second part covenants that he will pay to the party of the first part, for the use of said premises, the yearly rent of six hundred dollars, to be paid quarterly in advance, on the first days of July, October, January and April of each year.

Also that this lease shall not be assigned, nor the said premises, or any part thereof, underlet without the written consent of the said party of the first part, or his legal representatives, under penalty of forfeiture. And that all repairs of a temporary character, deemed necessary by said party of the second part, shall be made at his own expense, with the consent of the said party of the first part, or his legal representatives, and not otherwise.

And provided said party of the second part shall fail to pay said rent, or any part thereof, when it becomes due, it is agreed that said party of the first part may sue for the same, or re-enter said premises, or resort to any legal remedy.

The party of the second part agrees to pay all yearly city and county taxes to be assessed on said premises during said term.

The party of the second part covenants that, at the expiration of said term, he will surrender up said premises to the party of the first part in as good condition as now, necessary wear and damage by the elements excepted.

Witness the hands and seals of the said parties, the day and year first above written.

GEORGE L. WILLIAMS, [L. S.]

JAMES D. RANDALL. [L. S.]

In presence of

HENRY A. THOMAS.

WILL.

I, HENRY PARKER, of Washington, D. C., being of sound mind and memory and considering the uncertainty of this frail and transitory life, do therefore make, publish and declare this to be my last will and testament, that is to say:

First—After all my lawful debts are paid and discharged, I give and bequeath unto my wife, Mary Parker, the dwelling house and land connected therewith, which we now occupy as a homestead, and all other things used by us in housekeeping in connection therewith; also twenty-five shares in the Flour City National Bank.

Second—I give to my son John all my real estate in the town of Eden, Erie County, State of New York, and all the stock and implements used for farming purposes in connection with the same.

Third—I give to my daughter Jane five thousand dollars in cash for her sole use and for the use of her heirs, free from the control of her husband.

Fourth—The residue of my property, real and personal, I give and bequeath to my unfortunate invalid son, Walter.

Fifth—I hereby appoint my son John to be executor, and my wife Mary to be executrix, of this my last will and testament, hereby revoking all former wills by me made.

In witness whereof I have hereunto subscribed my name and affixed my seal the first day of June, in the year of our Lord one thousand, eight hundred and ninety.

HENRY PARKER. [L. S.]

The foregoing instrument was subscribed by the said Henry Parker in our presence, and acknowledged by him to each of us, and he at the same time declared the above instrument, so subscribed, to be his last will and testament; and we, at his request, have signed our names as witnesses hereto in his presence, and in the presence of each other, and written opposite our names our respective places of residence.

JOHN M. DUNNING,
10 14th St., Washington.
CALVIN TOWNSEND,
21 Penn. Ave., Washington.
NELSON L. BURTON,
27 8th St., Washington.

BUILDING CONTRACT.

Agreement made this fourth day of June, 1890, between Walter N. Clark, of Rochester, N. Y., of the first part, and Theodore C. Spencer, builder, of the same place, of the second part, the said party of the second part covenants to and with the said party of the first part, to make, erect, build, and finish in a good, substantial and workmanlike manner, on the lot belonging to the party of the first part, and known as No. 4 Bank Street, in said city of Rochester, one brick building, agreeably to the plans and specifications made by A. J. Warner, architect, hereto annexed, of good and substantial materials, by the first day of July next; and the said party of the first part cov-

(14)

enants and agrees to pay to the said party of the second part the sum of five thousand dollars, lawful money, in manner following: two thousand at the beginning of said work; two thousand dollars more when said house shall have been completely roofed, and one thousand dollars more in full for said work when the same shall be completely finished.

And for the true and faithful performance of each and all of the covenants and agreements above mentioned, the parties to these presents bind themselves, each unto the other, in the penal sum of one thousand dollars, as liquidated damages, to be paid by the failing party.

In witness whereof, we have hereunto signed our names and affixed our seals on the day and year first above written.

WALTER N. CLARK,   [L. S.]

THEODORE C. SPENCER. [L. S.]

Witness:

ARTHUR B. DIXON.

LESSON XLV.

SPECIFICATION FOR A BUILDING

To be Erected for the Rochester Machine Company, at Rochester, N. Y., according to following Specification and accompanying Drawings, prepared this 15th day of May, 1890, by A. J. Warner, Architect, Syracuse, N. Y.

General Description.

The building will be two stories in height. The first story will be ten feet in the clear at the lowest point, and the ceiling will rise the same slope as the roof.

The foundation will be stone.

The walls of superstructure will be brick with stone sills.

The roof will be of tin.

Location.

The building will be located upon the company's grounds as may be directed.

Excavation.

Excavate trenches for the walls and foundations for the columns six feet below the present grade line. The trenches must be eight inches wider than the wall.

As the walls are pointed up fill in against them, tamping the dirt in place and grading up to run all water away from the building.

Cart away all earth from the excavation not needed in grading up around the building.

FOUNDATION.

Mortar.—All mortar used must be composed of one-third fresh slaked lime, and two-thirds clean, sharp sand.

Build the walls as shown by the drawings, seven feet high; that is, they will extend from six feet below the grade line to one foot above. These walls will be built of first class rubble masonry, laid in lime mortar, using good-sized, regular-shaped sandstone, laid on their natural quarry beds, and all well slushed.

Point all walls up on both sides. Lay all walls to a line on both sides. At least one-fifth of these stones are to be headers, reaching through the wall.

Build the piers for the iron columns, putting in the footings as per drawings. These footing-stone are to be large size, not more than two stone to one footing.

The piers are to be laid up in regular courses, not less than nine inches high with pick-dressed joints and beds. The cap stone on the pier will be eighteen inches square with pick-dressed bed and chisel-dressed top.

Put in good sandstone door-sills, nine inches high, fourteen inches wide, six feet long.

Drill holes for flush bolts as directed by the carpenter.

WINDOW-SILLS.

All window-sills will be good quality of sandstone, drove dressed with corners perfect and surfaces straight. These sills will be four inch build, seven inch bed and eight inches longer than the opening. They will all be set with a projection of two inches and have a drip beneath.

BRICK-WORK.

Mortar.—All brick will be laid in first quality lime mortar, composed of one-third fresh slaked lime and two-thirds clean, sharp sand, mixed in a box and cooled five days before using.

Wetting Brick.—All brick must be wet immediately before laying.

Build all walls colored red on drawings to the top of the fire-wall, as shown on the drawings, of good, common brick, laid to a line on both sides, in good lime mortar; all brick must be well bedded, all joints well slushed, and brick well bonded, with headers every seventh course.

All exposed brick must be hard burned, of a uniform color.

The inside of walls will have the joints slushed full and the joints struck.

Fire-Wall.—The fire-wall will be carried up as per drawings, and will be nine inches thick.

Build in all joist, girders, window-frames and nogging, to secure tin work, as directed by the carpenter.

Window-Sills.—Carry up and set the window-sills.

PAINTING AND GLAZING.

Painting.—Kill all knots with shellac or silver-leaf before priming. Putty up all nail heads after priming.

Prime all door and window frames, including the backs, before they are set, and all other wood-work as it goes up.

Use yellow ocher and pure linseed oil for priming.

Paint all doors and door-frames, window-frames and sash three coats of such color as may be directed.

Paint the tin work one heavy coat in addition to what the tinner gives it.

Use no evaporating dryer on the outside.

Glazing.—Fill all sash with B. S. S. American blown glass. All glass must be bedded, bradded and puttied, back-set and cleaned of all lear smoke and left whole upon the completion of the building. Prime the sash before filling.

LESSON XLVI,

SPECIFICATION FOR A BUILDING—*Continued.*

TIN AND GALVANIZED IRON.

Tin.—Cover the roof and the inner side and top of the fire-walls with IX bright tin, M. F. brand.

This work will be all standing seam with 1½ and 1¼ inch tongueing, and all seams carefully double-folded and hammered down. Take care to leave tin free to expand and contract without breaking or loosening.

All tin must be painted two heavy coats on both sides before laying.

Galvanized Iron.—Put a galvanized iron hanging gutter in the rear, with six-inch galvanized-iron conductor to the ground. This gutter will be secured in place by galvanized wrought-iron bars one-sixteenth inch thick across the top of the gutter, secured to galvanized wrought-iron strips fastened to the roof.

WOOD-WORK.

Lintels.—All lintels over openings less than four feet will be two inches by four inches with one-inch blocks spiked between for proper thickness of wall. Lintels for openings four feet or over in width will be two inches by six inches, with one-inch blocks spiked between. Lintels must have a rest equal to the depth of the lintel.

Under the ends of the girders put four inch by eight inch by thirty-six inch oak plank. Put in wooden blocks that are necessary to secure the wood-work to the brick wall. Have blocks built in the top of the fire-wall to secure the sheeting for the tin-work. All lintels and nogging must be perfectly dry stuff.

Rough Sills.—In all windows put a rough sill under the frame, two inches by six inches, six inches longer than the width of opening.

Joist.—There will be no joist in the first story. The second-floor joist will be two inches by ten inches, sixteen inches from centers, all properly cambered and bridged with a row of double diagonal bridging to each length of joint. The second-story ceiling will be two inches by eight inches, two feet from centers.

Posts.—In the second story put in eight inch by eight inch posts to support the roof. These posts will extend down to the iron plate on top of the columns, and will have a four inch by eight inch by twenty-four inch bolster on top; bolster will be oak.

Girders.—Put in girders as shown by the drawing. Girder for second-story floor will be ten inches by fourteen inches; girder for the ceiling will be eight inches by twelve inches. These girders may be built up of two inch-plank, bolted together by five-eighth inch bolts, two feet from centers. These girders must have nine-inch rests on the walls.

Sheeting.—Cover the roof and fire-walls with seven-eighth inch stuff, dressed on one side, free from knot-holes and dead knots, laid close and well nailed, with nails driven well below the surface for tin work. Lay the dressed side down.

Rough Floor.—As soon as the joist are down for the second floor, lay a floor of seven-eighth inch stuff dressed on one side, the dressed side down, no board must exceed eight inches in width, and all lumber must be free from knot-holes and dead knots and shakes, and must present a neat appearance from the under side.

Window-Frames and Sash.—All window-frames will be one and three-eighth inch plank frames with sliding sash, with parting strips, etc., all complete. The sash will be one and three-eighth inches, and will have galvanized-iron spring-catches, two to each sash.

Door-Frames and Doors.—The door-frames will all be one and three-eighth inch by eight inches rabbeted frames.

The door in the second story will be a four-paneled ogee door, one and three-quarter inch thick, hung on three japanned loose-pin butts, and have mortised lock with thin steel keys and trimmings with black mineral knobs.

The doors in the first story will be made of two thicknesses of seven-eighth inch flooring, each side to run in the opposite direction, the dressed side to be out.

Each door will be hung on three, heavy, japanned, loose-pin butts. Two of these doors will be fastened on the inside with heavy oak bars in wrought-iron sockets. The other door will have a rim dead-lock furnished by the company and put on by the contractor. These doors will have top and bottom flush-bolts with heavy wrought-iron thumb-latches, handles, etc., complete.

Dressed Floor.—In the second story, after the sash are filled, cover the rough floor with a layer of tarred building-paper; over that lay a seven-eighth inch milled, matched, white-oak floor, secret nailed. No board must exceed six inches in width. This floor must be free from knots and all first quality.

Let the sheeting extend out over the wall in the rear at least four inches and put a seven-eighth inch board below as a finish on the end of the joist.

Iron Columns.—Furnish and set in place the iron columns in the first story. These columns must be long enough to make the second-story floor one inch higher in the center than at either side, to allow for shrinkage of girder. These columns will have bed plates one inch by twelve inches, cast with a ring to fit the column and be turned perfectly true. Make the casting on top of the column to receive the girders, as per drawings. This casting will be one-half inch metal, except the under part that is made to fit the column, which must be turned smooth, as well as the ends of the columns, to give a perfect bearing. This casting must have seven-eighth inch holes to receive three-quarter bolts passing through each girder.

LESSON XLVII.

COURT PROCEEDINGS.

IMPANELING OF A JURY.

The Court:

The jurors summoned will now be examined in order upon their *voire dire.*

WILLIAM B. TODD, sworn upon his *voire dire*, and examined as follows:

By the Court:

Q. Have you formed or expressed an opinion in regard to the guilt or innocence of the prisoner at the bar? A. To a certain extent I may have formed an opinion; I do not remember having expressed an opinion.

Q. Would that opinion have such an influence upon your judgment that you would not be able, upon the oath you have taken in consequence of such opinion, whatever may be the extent of it, to render a fair, honest and impartial verdict upon the evidence adduced on both sides in the trial? A. I do not think it would.

Q. Have you conscientious scruples against rendering a verdict of guilty in a case in which the punishment shall be death, provided the evidence should warrant you in finding such a verdict? A. None at all.

No challenge having been made, Mr. Todd was accordingly sworn in as a juror.

R. A. SHEPARD duly sworn and examined as follows:

By the Court:

Q. Have you formed or expressed an opinion in relation to the guilt or innocence of the prisoner at the bar? A. I have.

Q. You have both formed and expressed an opinion? A. Yes, sir.

Q. Under the oath you have taken, do you say to the Court that that opinion, as formed and expressed, would bias or prejudice your judgment in rendering a verdict as to the guilt or innocence of the prisoner, after having heard all the testimony in the case?   A. I fear it would, though I do not know what the evidence may be.

Q. Have you conscientious scruples against rendering a verdict of 'guilty in a case where the punishment is death, provided the evidence shall warrant you in such finding? A. Not in the least.

By the District Attorney:

Q. Where did you express this opinion?   A. While the trial was going on at the arsenal.

Q. Upon what evidence or what information was this opinion, which you expressed, based?   A. From reading the evidence on the trial of the others.

Q. Where did you read that evidence?   A. In a book published by the government; I have one of those books.

The Court: You may stand aside for the present.

ROBERT CORNELL duly sworn and examined as follows:

By the Court:

Q. Have you formed or expressed an opinion in relation to the guilt or innocence of the prisoner at the bar? A. I have probably given some expression of an impression formed upon my mind from common rumor, but I do not think that I have given any decided expression of opinion, nor have I formed any very decided opinion.

Q. From what you have seen and what you have heard in regard to these rumors, do you believe you would be able to render a fair and impartial verdict, after having heard all the testimony in the case? A. It is my impression I could do justice to the prisoner as well as to the state.

Q. Have you conscientious scruples against rendering a verdict of guilty in a case punishable with death, where the evidence would justify such finding? A. None whatever.

The Court decided Mr. Ball to be a competent juror, and no challenge being made, he was accordingly sworn as such.

THOMAS BARRYINGTON was called, and being duly sworn was examined as follows:

By the Court:

Q. Have you formed an opinion as to the guilt or innocence of the prisoner? A. I have.

Q. How and in what way did you form this opinion? A. From reading the statement of his arrest, and a portion of the proceedings on the trial of the other conspirators.

Q. Is the bias on your mind so strong as to prevent you doing impartial justice between the United States and the prisoner? A. No, sir.

Q. Do you think you could decide it fairly? A. Yes, sir; according to the law and the evidence.

Q. Have you any conscientious convictions as to the lawfulness of capital punishment? A. No, sir.

The Court: Gentleman, he is a competent juror.

Mr. Barryington: Permit me to say, your Honor, that I am not in very good health, and therefore do not know as I would be able to serve.

The Court: Have you a doctor's certificate?

Mr. Barryington: No, sir.

The Court: The presumption then is that you are able to serve.

Mr. Barryington, being accepted by counsel on either side, was sworn in by the Clerk:

JOHN H. CRANDELL was called, and being duly sworn was examined as follows:

By the Court:

Q. Have you formed an opinion as to the guilt or innocence of the prisoner at the bar? A. I have.

Q. In what way did you form this opinion? A. I formed the opinion from reading the report of the assassination trial two years ago, and from circumstances connected with the case.

Q. Is the bias on your mind so strong as to disable you from rendering an impartial verdict between the United States and the prisoner? A. No, sir.

Q. Do you believe you could decide according to the law and the evidence in the case? A. I think I could.

Q. Have you any conscientious convictions as to the lawfulness of capital punishment?. A. I am opposed to capital punishment.

Q. But so long as capital punishment is lawful by the laws of the land, would that disapprobation on your part influence you in rendering a verdict? A. It would not.

The Court: He is competent.

Challenged by the prisoner.

LESSON XLVIII.

COURT PROCEEDINGS—*Continued.*

Opening Address to the Jury for the Plaintiff.

Monday, June 18, 1867.

Criminal Court—Associate Justice Fisher, presiding.

The court opened at ten o'clock A.M.   The Clerk proceeded to call the names of the jury impaneled on Saturday, all of whom responded.

Mr. Nathaniel Wilson, Assistant District Attorney, then addressed the jury as follows:

May it please your Honor and gentlemen of the jury, you are doubtless aware that it is customary in criminal cases for the prosecution, at the beginning of a trial, to inform the jury of the nature of the offense to be inquired into, and of the proof that will be offered in support of the charges of the indictment.   By making such a statement I hope to aid you in clearly ascertaining the work that is before us, and in apprehending the relevancy and significance of the testimony that will be produced as the case proceeds.

The grand jury of the District of Columbia have indicted the prisoner at the bar, John H. Surratt, as one of the murderers of Abraham Lincoln.   It has become your duty to judge whether he be guilty or innocent of that charge—a duty than which one more solemn or momentous never was committed to human intelligence. You are to turn back the leaves of history to that red page on which is recorded in letters of blood the awful incidents of that April night on which the assassin's work was done on the body of the Chief Magistrate of the American Republic—a night on which for the first time in our existence as a nation a blow was struck with the fell purpose of destroying not only human life, but the life of the nation, the life of liberty itself. Though more than two years have passed by since then, you scarcely need witnesses to describe to you the scene in Ford's Theater as it was visible in the last hour of the President's conscious life. It has been present to your thoughts a thousand times since then. A vast audience was assembled, whose hearts were throbbing with a new joy, born of victory and peace, and above them the object of their gratitude and reverence—he who had borne the nation's burdens through many and disastrous years—sat tranquil and at rest at last, a victor indeed, but a victor in whose generous heart triumph awakened no emotions save those of kindness, of forgiveness, and of charity. To him, in that hour of supreme tranquillity, to him in the charmed circle of friendship and affection, there came the form of sudden and terrible death.

Persons who were then present will tell you that about twenty minutes past ten o'clock that night, the night of the 14th of April, 1865, John Wilkes Booth, armed with

(15)

pistol and knife, passed rapidly from the front door of the theater, ascended to the dress circle, and entered the President's box. By the discharge of a pistol he inflicted the death wound, then leaped upon the stage, and passing rapidly across it, disappeared into the darkness of the night.

We shall prove to your entire satisfaction, by competent and credible witnesses, that at that time the prisoner at the bar was then present, aiding and abetting that murder, and that at twenty minutes past ten o'clock that night he was in front of that theater in company with Booth. You shall hear what he then said and did. You shall know that his cold and calculating malice was the director of the bullet that pierced the brain of the President and the knife that fell upon the face of the venerable Secretary of State. You shall know that the prisoner at the bar was the contriver of that villainy, and that from the presence of the prisoner, Booth, drunk with theatric passion and traitorous hate, rushed directly to the execution of their mutual will.

'We shall further prove to you that their companionship upon that occasion was not an accidental nor an unexpected one, but that the butchery that ensued was the ripe result of a long premeditated plot, in which the prisoner was the chief conspirator. It will be proved to you that he is a traitor to the government that protected him; a spy in the employ of the enemies of his country in the years 1864 and 1865, passed repeatedly from Richmond to Washington, from Washington to Canada, weaving the web of his nefarious scheme, plotting the overthrow of this government, the defeat of its armies, and the slaughter of his countrymen; and as showing the venom of his intent—as showing a mind insensible to every moral obligation and fatally bent on mischief—we shall prove his gleeful boasts that during these journeys he had shot down in cold blood weak and unarmed Union soldiers fleeing from Rebel prisons. It will be proved to you that he made his home in this city the rendezvous for the tools and agents in what he called his "bloody work," and that his hand provided and deposited at Surrattsville, in a convenient place, the very weapons obtained by Booth while escaping, one of which fell or was wrenched from Booth's death-grip at the moment of his capture.

While in Montreal, Canada, where he had gone from Richmond on the 10th of April, the Monday before the assassination, Surratt received a summons from his co-conspirator, Booth, requiring his immediate presence in this city. In obedience to that preconcerted signal he at once left Canada, and arrived here on the 13th. By numerous, I had almost said a multitude of witnesses, we shall make the proof to be as clear as the noon-day sun, and as convincing as the axioms of truth, that he was here during the day of that fatal Friday, as well as present at the theater that night, as I have before stated. We shall show him to you on Pennsylvania Avenue, booted and spurred, awaiting the arrival of the fatal moment. We shall show him in conference with Herold in the evening;

we shall show him purchasing a contrivance for disguise an hour or two before the murder.

When the last blow had been struck, when he had done his utmost to bring anarchy and desolation upon his native land, he turned his back upon the abomination he had wrought, he turned his back upon his home and kindred, and commenced his shuddering flight.

LESSON XLIX.

COURT PROCEEDINGS—*Continued.*

We shall trace that flight, because in law flight is the criminal's inarticulate confession, and because it happened in this case, as it always happens, and always must happen, that in some moment of fear, or of elation, or of fancied security, he, too, to others, confessed his guilty deeds.   He fled to Canada.   We will prove to you the hour of his arrival there, and the route he took.   He there found safe concealment, and remained there several months, voluntarily absenting himself from his mother.   In the following September he again took flight.   Still in disguise, with painted face and painted hair and painted hand, he took ship to cross the Atlantic.   In mid-ocean he revealed himself and related his exploits, and spoke freely of his connection with Booth in the conspiracy relating to the President.   He rejoiced in the death of the President; he lifted his impious hand to heaven and expressed the wish that he might live to return to America and serve Andrew Johnson as Abraham Lincoln had been served.   He was hidden for a time in England, and found there sympathy and hospitality; but soon was made again an outcast and a wanderer by his guilty secret.   From England he went to Rome, and hid himself in the ranks of the Papal army in the guise of a private soldier.   Having placed almost the diameter of the globe between himself and the dead

body of his victim, he might well fancy that pursuit was
baffled; but by the happening of one of those events
which we sometimes call accidents, but which are indeed
the mysterious means by which Omniscient and Omnipo-
tent Justice reveals and punishes the doers of evil, he was
discovered by an acquaintance of his boyhood. /When
denial would not avail he admitted his identity, and avowed
his guilt in these memorable words: "I have done the
Yankees as much harm as I could. We have killed Lincoln, the niggers' friend." The man to whom Surratt
made this statement did as it was his high duty to do—he
made known his discovery to the American minister.
There is no treaty of extradition with the Papal states;
but so heinous is the crime with which Surratt is charged,
such bad notoriety had his name obtained, that his
Holiness the Pope and Cardinal Antonelli ordered his
arrest without waiting for a formal demand from the
American Government. Having been arrested, he escaped
from his guards by a leap down a precipice—a leap impossible to any one but one to whom conscience made life
valueless. He made his way to Naples, and then took
passage in a steamer that carried him across the Mediter-
ranean Sea to Alexandria, in Egypt. He was pursued,
not by the "blood-hounds of the law" that seem to haunt
the imagination of the prisoner's counsel, but by the very
elements, by destruction itself, made a bond-slave in the
service of justice.) The inexorable lightning thrilled along
the wires that stretch through the waste of waters that
roll between the shores of Italy and the shores of Egypt

and spoke in his ear its word of terrible command, and from Alexandria, aghast and manacled, he was made to turn his face towards the land he had polluted by the curse of murder. He is here at last to be tried for this crime.

And when the facts which I have stated have been proved, as proved they assuredly will be if anything is ever proved by human testimony; and when all the subterfuges of the defense have been disproved, as disproved they assuredly will be, we, having done our duty in furnishing you with that proof of the prisoner's guilt, in the name of the civilization he has dishonored, in the name of the country he has betrayed and disgraced, in the name of the law he has violated and defied, shall demand of you that retribution, though tardily, shall yet be surely done upon the shedder of innocent and precious blood.

WILLIAM J. WHITE, sworn for the people:

Direct examination by Mr. Quinby:

Q. Mr. White, where do you live? A. In the city of Buffalo.

Q. What is your business? A. Civil engineer.

Q. How long have you been a civil engineer? A. About six years.

Q. Did you make this map? A. I did, sir.

Q. When did you go down to the premises first for the purpose of taking your measurements? A. On March 29, 1889.

Q. At the right of your map, facing it, what does it represent? A. It represents the premises, 526 South Division Street, and the adjoining buildings shown in sections—parts of them.

Q. South Division Street runs in what direction? A. Nearly east and west.

Q. These premises in question are situated upon which side of South Division Street? A. North side.

Q. The house in front is made of what material? A. Wood.

Q. And of how many stories? A. Two—a portion of it.

Q. Running back to the portion in the rear, of how many stories? A. One.

Q. It fronts upon South Division Street? A. Yes, sir.

ROSWELL F. PARK, M. D., affirmed for the people.

Direct examination by Mr. Quinby:

Q. You live in Buffalo? A. Yes, sir.

Q. Practicing physician and surgeon? A. Yes, sir.

Q. And have been for how many years? A. Thirteen or fourteen years.

Q. What institutions, if any, are you connected with? A. The Medical Department of the University of Buffalo, General Hospital, Fitch Hospital.

Q. Your specialty is surgery? A. Yes, sir.

Q. You have had some experience in head wounds, fractures of the skull? A. Yes, sir.

LESSON L.

COURT PROCEEDINGS—*Continued.*

Tell the jury about how many cases have come under your observation, of fractures and incised bones upon the head; some idea of your experience? A. Well, I have no idea, sir; I have seen a good many hundred of them.

Q. Did you see the woman called Matilda Ziegler or Hort at the Fitch Hospital? A. I did; yes, sir.

Q. When was it that you saw her first, Doctor? A. I think it was March 29th.

Q. About what time of day? A. About eleven; between eleven and twelve, as nearly as I can recollect.

Q. In the daytime? A. Yes, sir.

Q. At the Fitch Hospital? A. Yes, sir.

Q. Where was she when you first saw her? A. She was lying on the operating table there.

Q. Who was present at the time? A. Dr. Jones and the nurse, Mr. Corlett, one of the resident students there; I do not recall who else. I know there were several there.

Q. Was the woman conscious or unconscious? A. Unconscious.

Q. Describe, Doctor, the condition that you found her in, as to the injuries upon her person. A. I found her with a large number of rough scalp wounds, lacerated skull wounds, and of course head covered with blood, more or less, and bruised and disfigured.

Q. What did you do?   A. I had chloroform given to her and I operated upon her.

Q. Describe the operation and what the result was? A. Well, there was one point on, I think, the left side of her head where evidently the skull had been driven in, or depressed, as we say; and I cut through the scalp over that part and found several pieces of bone that were entirely loose, pieces of the skull, and removed them, and I stopped the bleeding and closed the wound.

Q. What was the object of this?   A. To save her life, if possible.

Q. To remove the pressure from the brain?   A. Yes, sir.

Q. Before this did you discover whether any portion of the brain proper was oozing out?   A. Yes, it was.

Q. What part of the brain was it that oozed out?   A. About this portion (indicates), what we call the cerebrum.

Q. Left?   A. Left side, I think.

Q. Left side of the head and nearly above the ear? A. Yes, sir.

Q. Could you tell me from the examination of this wound whether the fracture was made by a sharp or a blunt instrument?   A. I should say by a blunt instrument.

Q. Were there any wounds upon the head that indicated them to have been made by a sharp instrument? A. Nothing that I recall. Everything had the appearance to me of having been done by some blunt instrument; it was not clean cut.

Q. Did you take any notice to count the number of wounds upon the head? A. I did not.

Q. What other fracture of the skull, if any, did you find other than you have described? A. Why, this was a complicated fracture; its lines ran in two or three different directions.

Q. And branching out from a common center? A. Yes, sir.

Q. What was the length of the radiations? A. I did not follow them clear out; it would have involved too much investigation, more than I thought was proper in the case; what I paid special attention to was to see if the bone was driven below its proper level; that was the most important part first.

Q. Did any of the fractures extend to the frontal bone? A. Yes, sir.

Q. Or front portion of the head? A. Yes, around in that direction.

Q. Any toward the rear did you notice? A. I think so; it was a radiating fracture as we should say.

Q. What are the names of the bones of the head that were fractured that you saw? A. It was mainly in the parietal bone; parietal and temporal bones.

Q. Was this a normal skull, Doctor, as to thickness? A. So far as I saw; yes, sir.

Q. You may state to the jury whether or not this was a serious wound. A. Very; I regarded it as fatal when I saw it.

Q. Did you perform any other operation than the ones you have described? A. That is all.

Q. Did you see her subsequently? A. No, sir.

Q. She was dead? A. She died, I understood, that night.

Q. You never saw her again alive? A. No, sir.

Q. You knew the fact that she did die? A. I was told so.

Q. You were so informed that she did die? A. Yes, sir.

Q. A blow upon the head in the locality you have described, by an instrument of this nature (referring to hatchet), you may state whether or not it would be dangerous to 'human life? A. Depend entirely upon the—

Q. To strike a person on the head with an instrument similar to this that I have in my hand in the locality in which you found this injury? A. It certainly is dangerous.

Q. To human life? A. Yes, sir.

Cross examination by Mr. Sickmon:

Q. How old a woman did this appear to be, Doctor? A. I thought between thirty and thirty-five.

Q. About what was her height? A. I should have to guess at it.

Q. Yes, give us your best judgment. A. About five feet six, I should say.

LESSON LI.

COURT PROCEEDINGS—*Continued.*

JOHN R. KENNEY, sworn for the people.

Direct examination by Mr. Quinby:

Q. Mr. Kenney, you are the coroner of this county?
A. I am.

Q. You had charge of the case of Matilda Ziegler?
A. I did.

Q. Where did you first see her? A. At the Fitch Accident Hospital.

Q. What time and on what day? A. I was called there, over the telephone, about ten o'clock in the morning —on Friday morning, the 29th day of March last, to take an ante-mortem statement.

Q. You did not take the statement? A. I did not.

Q. Why? A. She was not in condition; unconscious.

Q. You never took her statement? A. I never did.

Q. Did you afterwards see her dead body? A. I did.

Q. Where did you remove it to? A. To the morgue.

Q. Where is the morgue situated? A. The morgue is situated on the Terrace in the rear of the jail.

Q. Who made the post-mortem examination? A. Dr. Henry Bingham.

Q. And upon the body of Matilda Ziegler? A. Yes, sir.

Q. When did he make that examination? A. On Saturday morning, Saturday forenoon, the 30th of March last.

Q. After the post-mortem examination the body was buried? A. Yes, sir.

Q. By whom? A. By Crowley Brothers.

DANIEL E. BARRY, sworn for the people.

Direct examination by Mr. Quinby:

Q. You are a member of the Buffalo police force, Captain? A. Yes, sir.

Q. What precinct are you captain of? A. Number Two.

Q. You recollect the morning of the 29th of March? A. Yes, sir.

Q. About what time did you get any word at the Police Station of the affray? A. I got word at police headquarters about quarter past nine.

Q. You got your news from police headquarters? A. Yes, sir.

Q. What time did you get to the station-house that morning? A. Ten o'clock.

Q. Was Kemmler there when you got there? A. He was.

Q. Where was he when you first saw him? A. He was locked up in the cell department.

Q. Did you notice his personal appearance that morning? A. Yes, sir.

Q. How was he, sober? A. Yes, sir; he was.

Q. Now tell the jury what took place between you and him? A. I went into the cell department and he was sitting on far side of the cell; when I called him he came to the door, and I asked him if he wanted to make a statement; he said no, he did not want to.

WILLIAM D. REILLY, sworn for the people.

Direct examination by Mr. Quinby:

Q. You live in Buffalo? A. I do.

Q. What is your business? A. I am in the fruit and commission business on the Elk Street Market.

Q. How long have you been in the fruit and commission business? A. About nine years.

Q. Do you know the defendant, Kemmler? A. I do.

Q. How long have you known him? A. I have known him perhaps little more than a year.

Q. Have you seen him there at the market? A. I have.

Q. Has he traded with you? A. He has at different times ; yes.

Q. Purchased fruit or something of you? A. Fruit, yes ; always fruit.

Q. Did he ever come in your place and sit down? A. No.

Q. Talk with you? A. No.

Q. Did you ever see him sitting around any place? A. I do not know that I have ; I do not ever remember of having seen him sitting around any place.

Q. Did he pay cash or run an account there? A. He usually paid cash ; in fact he always paid cash.

Q. Who did the figuring as to what he was to pay generally? A. Well, he always did his cash business with my book-keeper, and I guess there have been two or three times when he left a small balance, but always paid it promptly.

Q. Outside of this intoxication that has been spoken of, did you notice anything out of the way in any way? A. No.

Cross examination by Mr. Sickmon:

Q. Where did you first get acquainted with the defendant? A. I remember the first time that I ever saw him was on the market about a year ago; perhaps a little more than a year ago.

Q. Did your dealings with him extend during all the time that you have known him; did they commence shortly after you met him on the market? A. Yes, sir.

Q. The dealings which you had were in your place? A. Yes, sir; in my store.

Q. Has he been in there intoxicated? A. Well, I do not know that I have ever seen him in my place intoxicated; I have seen him around the market, though, at different times intoxicated.

Q. So that he staggered? A. Well, yes; he staggered; you could see that he was drunk.

Q. Was his face flushed? A. Well, yes.

Q. He had the evidence of being a hard drinker, did he not, upon his countenance? A. He always impressed me as being a hard drinker; yes, sir.

Mr. Quinby: That is our case.

Adjourned until May 8, 1889, 9.30 A. M.

LESSON LII.

ADDRESS TO THE JURY FOR THE DEFENDANT.

EXTRACT OF ARGUMENT BY D. W. VOORHEES, DE-
LIVERED AT CHARLESTON, VA., NOVEMBER 8,
1859, UPON THE TRIAL OF JOHN E. COOK,
INDICTED FOR TREASON, MURDER AND
INCITING SLAVES TO REBEL AT THE
HARPER'S FERRY INSURRECTION.

With the permission of the Court:

GENTLEMEN OF THE JURY: The place I occupy in standing before you at this time is one clothed with a responsibility as weighty and as delicate as was ever assigned an advocate in behalf of an unfortunate fellow-man. No language that I can employ could give an additional force to the circumstances by which I am surrounded, and which press so heavily on the public mind as well as on my own. I come, too, as a stranger to each one of you. Your faces I know only by the common image we bear to our Maker; but in your exalted character of citizens of the ancient and proud Commonwealth of Virginia and of the American Union, I bear to you a passport of friendship and letter of introduction. I come from the sunset side of your western mountains, from beyond the rivers that now skirt the borders of your great state; but I come not as an alien to a

(16)

foreign land, but rather as one who returns to the home of his ancestors and to the household from which he sprang. I come here not as an enemy, but as a friend, with interest common with yourselves, hoping for your hopes, and praying that the prosperity and glory of Virginia may be perpetual. Nor do I forget that the very soil on which I live in my western home was once owned by this venerable commonwealth, as much as the soil on which I now stand. Her laws there once prevailed, and all her institutions were there established as they are here. Not only my own state of Indiana, but also four other great states in the northwest stand as enduring and lofty monuments of Virginia's magnanimity and princely liberality. Her donation to the general government made them sovereign states; and since God gave the fruitful land of Canaan to Moses and Israel, such a gift of present and future empire has never been made to any people. Coming from the bosom of one of these states, can I forget the fealty and duty which I owe to the supremacy of your laws, the sacredness of your citizenship, or the sovereignty of your state? Rather may the child forget its parent and smite with unnatural hand the author of its being.

I am not here, gentlemen, in behalf of this pale-faced, fair-haired wanderer from his home and the paths of duty, to talk to you about the cold technicalities of the law, born of laborious analysis by the light of the midnight lamp. I place him before you on no such narrow grounds. He is in the hands of friends who abhorred the conduct of which he has been guilty. But does that fact debar him of human sympathy? Does the sinful act smite the erring brother with the leprosy which forbids the touch of the hand of affection? Is his voice of repentance, an appeal for forgiveness, stifled in his mouth? If so, the meek Savior of the world would have recoiled with horror from Mary Magdalene, and spurned the repentant sorrow of Peter, who denied him.

If He who made the earth, and hung the sun and moon and stars on high to give it light, and created man a joint heir of eternal wealth, and put within him an immortal spark of that celestial frame which surrounds His throne, could remember mercy in executing justice, when His whole plan of divine government was assailed and degraded; when His law was set at defiance and violated; when the purity of Eden had been defiled by the presence and counsels of the serpent—why, so can you, and so can I, when the wrong and the crime stand confessed, and every atonement is made to the majesty of the law, which the prisoner has in his power to make.

Gentlemen, you have the case. I surrender into your hands the issue of life and death. As long as you live, a more important case than this you will never be called to try. Consider it, therefore, well in all its bearings. I have tried to show you those facts which go to palliate the conduct of the prisoner. Shall I go home and say that in justice you remembered not mercy to him? Leave the door of clemency open; do not shut it by wholesale conviction. Remember that life is an awful and sacred thing; remember that death is terrible, terrible at any time and in any form. But when to the frightful mien of the grim monster, when to the chilled visage of the spirit of the glass and scythe, is added the hated, dreaded specter of the gibbet, we turn shuddering from the accumulated horror. God spare this boy and those that love him from such a scene of woe. I part from you now, and most likely forever. When we next meet, when next I look upon your faces and you on mine, it will be in that land and before that tribunal where the only plea that will save you or me from a worse fate than awaits the prisoner will be mercy. Charity is the paramount virtue; all else is as sounding brass and a tinkling cymbal. Charity suffereth long, and is kind. Forbid it not to come into your deliberations; and, when your last hour comes, the memory that you allowed it to plead for your erring brother, John E. Cook, will brighten your passage over the dark river and rise by your side as an interceding angel in that day when your trial, as well as his, shall be determined by a just but merciful God. I thank the Court, and you, gentlemen, for your patient kindness, and I am done.

LESSON LIII.

COURT PROCEEDINGS—*Continued.*

RICHARD COLLINS, sworn for the defendant.

Direct examination by Mr. Sickmon:

Q. You are a door-man at Station One, Mr. Collins?
A. Yes, sir.

Q. And were March last? A. Yes, sir.

Q. Do you know the defendant, Kemmler? A. Yes, I know him.

Q. He was confined for a time in Police Station Number One? A. Yes, sir.

Q. Do you recollect when he was brought there. A. Yes, sir.

Q. What day of the month? A. I don't know the date or the day, but I know it was in the night time; about, I guess, the first time I saw him was between nine and ten o'clock.

Q. You recollect the day of the killing? A. I do; yes, sir.

Q. Was it the evening of that day that he was brought to the station? A. I think it was.

Q. Were you on duty at the time he was brought there? A. Yes, sir.

Q. And your hours are from—? A. Well, they were from four to twelve that week; we change.

Q. They change from week to week? A. Yes, sir.

Q. From four o'clock in the afternoon until—? A. Twelve at night.

Q. By whom was he brought to Station Number One? A. Well, when I was home he was in charge of Lieutenant Barry—Number Two.

Q. Did Barry come over with him? A. I don't know; he came down stairs with him from the Superintendent's office, I believe.

Q. Was there some liquor procured for Kemmler that night? A. Yes, sir.

Q. Who got it? A. I got it.

Q. Where did you obtain the liquor? A. At Alderman Davy's, on the corner.

Q. John Davy? A. Yes, sir.

Q. How much did you get? A. I got a pop-bottle full of whisky and a half-dozen good cigars for him.

Q. Did you get any other liquor for him? A. That is all that I got.

Q. What was done with this liquor that you got? A. It was given to Kemmler.

Q. Was the bottle passed in to him? A. No, sir; given to him gradually.

Q. The whole of it? A. No; well, we gave him a drink along as we thought he needed it, or when he asked for it, once in awhile.

Q. And there was other liquor sent for, was there not? A. There was other liquor got, too.

Q. You did not get that? A. No, sir; I told the door-man that relieved me, on the orders that I got.

Q. From whom did you receive your orders? A. From O'Brian.

Q. Who is he? A. He is the Superintendent's operator; operator at headquarters.

Q. You left orders to the door-man who succeeded you to procure him some more liquor? A. Well, he hadn't drank what I got him; I told him to give him that, as I was ordered to give it to him.

T. D. CROTHERS, M. D., sworn for the defendant.

Direct examination by Mr. Sickmon:

Q. Where do you reside? A. Hartford, Conn.

Q. Are you connected with any institution at present? A. Yes, sir; with an inebriate asylum there.

Q. An inebriate asylum located where? A. In Hartford, Conn.

Q. What is it called? A. Walnut Lodge.

Q. Are you a physician? A. Yes, sir.

Q. In charge of that institution? A. In charge of the institution.

Q. Were you formerly a physician of the inebriate asylum at Binghamton? A. Yes, sir.

Q. When? A. I was assistant physician from 1872 to 1877.

Q. Besides being connected with the institution which you have named what other occupation have you? A. Well, I am editor of a journal devoted to the discussion of disease; of the disease of drink and of drinking men; and make that a specialty, the scientific study of drinking men and the literature on the subject.

Q. And the effects of it?   A. Yes, sir; and the effects of alcohol on the brain.

Q. How many years have you had charge of this journal; been editor of it?   A. Thirteen years.

Q. What is the name of this journal?   A. *Journal of Inebriety*.

Q. Since your connection with the inebriate asylum at Binghamton, down to the present time, have you made the study of inebriety and its effects upon the brain and morals of the person using intoxicating liquors a study? A. Yes, sir, I have.

Q. For how many years have you made that study a specialty?   A. About fourteen—fifteen years; fifteen years since I began to study that specialty.

Q. During that time have you, examined large numbers of individuals who suffered from the excessive use of alcohol?   A. Yes, sir, very large numbers.

Q. About what number?   A. Oh, I have seen twenty-five hundred or three thousand cases, probably.

Q. Will you state the effects of alcohol upon the brain and the physical system generally?   A. A man who uses alcohol to excess, as a rule, has a defective brain.   The first effect of alcohol stimulates the heart and brain, and the second effect paralyzes it.   So that a man after using alcohol awhile has a defective brain, a paralyzed brain, a brain incompetent to decide on the relations of life and all the finer conditions. That is the general effect. It produces a species of degeneration—brain degeneration—particularly in persons who use it to excess and continuously, for any length of time.

Q. What is the effect upon the moral sense? A. Destroys a man's character; destroys his veracity; destroys his power of judging right from wrong, and particularly his veracity and his comprehension of right and wrong, and power of discrimination between good and evil. The degeneration affects the morals quite as much as it does the body and brain.

Q. How does it affect the physical system? A. Not so markedly. It affects the physical system in some degree, but not so marked as it does the brain and nervous system.

Q. What effect does it have upon the will power? A. It lessens—destroys the will power; makes a man incapable of doing what he would do if he had not taken the spirits; destroys his will power; breaks it up.

Q. Take, for instance, a man whose father drank to excess and was drunk every week, and whose mother died with consumption, what would you say as to the probability of such a man inheriting a weak and excitable nervous system and weak brain?

Mr. Quinby: To that I object. There is no evidence here that Kemmler's father drank prior to the time of his birth. The boy says that he only knew when he was ten years of age that his father was a drinking man.

The Court: Yes, that is true; nothing here to indicate that Kemmler's father ever drank any liquor until long after Kemmler was born.

Q. What effect would the fact of his mother being a consumptive have upon the descendant? A. Consumption and drinking are very closely related.

LESSON LIV.

COURT PROCEEDINGS—*Continued.*

Cross examination by Mr. Quinby:

Q. Did you say that you were connected with an asylum? A. Yes, sir.

Q. In Connecticut? A. Yes, sir.

Q. Is that a private or public—? A. Private asylum.

Q. Who got that asylum started? A. A company.

Q. It is a stock company? A. Yes, sir.

Q. You are one of the—? A. I am one of the stockholders.

Q. ——incorporators? A. Yes, sir.

Q. And you are the head of it? A. Yes, sir.

Q. It is a business enterprise; is not in charge of any officers of the state? A. No, sir.

Q. You are the originator, are you not, of what is termed— of what you call " alcoholic insanity?" A. No, sir; no, sir.

Q. Are you not the man who has written a book on alcoholic insanity? A. No, sir.

Q. Are you not the Doctor Crothers? A. I am a Doctor Crothers; yes, sir.

Q. Are you not the man who wrote the book? A. The book was written fifty years ago on the subject. I am a man who defended the theory.

Q. This journal— you publish that journal, do you not?   A. Yes, sir.

Q. In connection with this stock company?   A. Yes, sir.

Q. And it is for the purpose of advertising among some things, is it not, your institution?   A. No, sir.

Q. Is not that one of its objects?   A. Not at all.

Q. Don't you advertise your institution in it?   A. I do, and I advertise all other institutions in this country.

Q. I ask you the question now; just confine yourself, please.   A. Yes, sir; certainly.

Q. You advertise your institution in your journal?   A. Yes, sir.

Q. When did you first contemplate being a witness in this case?   A. About two weeks ago, I think.

Q. Had you ever seen the defendant at that time?   A. No, sir.

A. Had anything been submitted to you in his case?   A. Yes, sir.

Q. What? . A. Well, the supposed evidence; the evidence that had been taken on the coroner's inquest.

Q. Of what? Of his drunkenness? A. Of his drunkenness.

Q. Anything more?   A. Of his general history.

Q. What was the general history?   A. That of continuous drunkenness, and the character of the crime, and the condition at the time of the crime.

Q. The condition at the time of the crime?   A. Yes, sir.

Q. We will get at that in a moment. You are in conflict with many of the recognized standard authors upon this question of alcoholic insanity, are you not? A. I do not think I am; no, sir.

Q. Do the standard authors claim that there is anything of alcoholic insanity, beyond the mere fact that it may produce a disease of the brain, the same as other things may produce a disease of the brain, which leads to insanity? A. That is my view. That is the view of the standard authors.

Q. That there are various things that may produce a disease of the brain? A. Certainly.

Q. What is insanity? A. Disease of the brain.

.Q. Evincing itself how? A. By irregular acts; irregular conduct and thoughts, and so on.

Q. Out of what we call the ordinary? A. Yes, sir; out of the ordinary

Q. What particular definition would you give to insanity produced by alcohol? A. Nothing more than alcoholic insanity.

Q. Is it dementia? A. No, sir; not specifically.

Q. It is not dementia? A. Not specifically; no, sir.

Q. What are the larger divisions of insanity? A. Well, there is mania; there is dementia; there is melancholia; those are some of the divisions.

Q. I do not understand you to say that this man is insane, do you? A. No, sir; I did not say that he was insane.

Q. Then upon your mere knowledge that he had been

a hard drinking man, you come to testify as to his inability; is that true? A. Supposing the facts that had been presented to me were true; supposing they were to be true.

Q. Well, he told you the facts; of his hard drinking? A. Yes, sir.

Q. And upon the mere fact òf his hard drinking, you come here to be a witness to swear to his inability, is that true? A. Certainly, it is.

Q. What time did you get to the jail this morning? A. About nine; perhaps half past eight.

Q. About how lóng before nine o'clock? A. Oh, perhaps half past eight.

Q. And how long was your examination? A. Oh, fifteen or twenty minutes; or, perhaps half an hour; something like that.

Q. Well, fifteen, twenty minutes or a half-hour? A. Yes, sir.

Q. What ground did you go over with him; tell the jury? A. Nothing except to look at the man and hear what he had to state, and ask him some questions; and note his mental capacity of answering.

Q. What questions were asked him, and what answers were made? A. I asked him about his memory.

Q. Give us the questions and answers? A. I cannot specify every question again.

Q. Give us one question? A. I asked him about his memory; I asked him if he had a good memory; he said he did not.

Q. Whether that was true or not you do not know?
A. No, sir, I do not.

Q. You knew the man was on trial here for a serious crime, did you not? A. Yes, sir.

Q. Did you test his memory by any specific question? A. No, sir; I asked him generally about it.

Q. What was the first question you asked him about committing the crime? A. I asked him if he remembered the circumstances of the crime.

Q. What did he say to that? You say he hesitated. A. He hesitated. Finally, after pressing the question, in two or three different ways, he said he thought not. He thought he did not remember it. That is his answer? A. Yes, sir.

Q. You took his word for that? A. I have no reason to doubt or disbelieve him.

Q. You are one of the people who believe in insane impulses? A. Certainly I do.

Q. What you call an insane impulse is an uncontrollable impulse, is it not? A. Certainly.

Re-direct examination by Mr. Sickmon:

Q. This impulse that you have spoken of was induced by a defective brain? A. Certainly.

Re-cross examination by Mr. Quinby:

Q. All brains are more or less defective, are they not? A. Not necessarily; no, sir.

Q. How is it generally speaking? A. A man who drinks whisky has a defective brain, of course.

Q. Any man who drinks any amount of whisky has a defective brain? A. Yes, sir.

Re-direct examination by Mr. Sickmon:

Q. And the more they drink, the more they are—? A. The worse they are; yes, sir.

Mr. Sickmon: We rest.

Evidence closed.

Recess until two o'clock.

LESSON LV.

COURT PROCEEDINGS—*Continued.*

CHARGE TO THE JURY.

Gentlemen of the Jury:

The defendant has been indicted and placed upon his trial for the crime of murder in killing Matilda Zeigler, in this city, on the 29th day of March last.

Gentlemen, the statute provides that the killing of a human being, unless it is excusable or justifiable, is murder in the first degree when committed, either from a deliberate and premeditated design to effect the death of the person killed, or of another; or by an act imminently dangerous to others, and evincing a depraved mind, regardless of human life, although without a premeditated design to effect the death of any individual; or without a design to effect death by a person engaged in the commission of, or in an attempt to commit a felony, either upon or affecting the person killed, or otherwise; or, third, when perpetrated in committing the crime of arson in the first degree.

There is no suggestion that the offense committed in taking the life of this woman would fall in any other than the first degree, as defined by this part of the statute, if it fall within any one of the provisions of this section.

(17)

The statute further provides that the killing of a
human being, unless it is excusable or justifiable, is
murder in the second degree when committed with a design to affect the death of the person killed, or of another,
but without deliberation or premeditation. And further
provides that such killing is manslaughter in the first
degree when committed without a design to effect death,
or by a person engaged in committing or attempting to
commit a misdemeanor, etc.

It is probably unnecessary to call your attention to
further definitions of the different degrees of homicide.
It is divided into murder in the first degree, into murder
in the second degree and into the different degrees of
manslaughter. It is not suggested that if a crime was
committed in depriving this woman of her life, that it
falls within either of the degrees of manslaughter.

Now, gentlemen, the killing being conceded by the
defendant; being admitted, and it not being claimed that
it was justifiable or excusable in the defendant to deprive
this woman of her life, your attention is directed to the
question which you are to pass upon; and the first question is, was the killing of this woman, under the circumstances detailed in the evidence, a criminal act? And, in
the second place, if it was a criminal act, what crime was
the defendant guilty of in depriving this woman of her
life?

Upon the first proposition in the case — was it a
criminal act?—your attention is directed to the testimony
as to the mental condition of this man. There is evidence

in the case from which it is claimed by the defense that this man was so far alienated mentally that he was labor-ing under such an enfeebled condition of mind as to be irresponsible for any act which he could do. The rule of law which would govern in this or in any other criminal case, is that a person must possess sufficient mind to be able to understand the nature and quality of the act, and he must be able to understand that the act is wrong. If his mind is in such a condition, from disease or from any other cause, that he is unable to understand that the act for which he is placed upon his trial is wrong; if he was unable to understand the nature and quality of that act, he is irresponsible, and in every such case as that it must result in a verdict of acquittal. But if he did under-stand the nature and quality of the act; of this killing; if he knew that it was wrong to take this woman's life, then he is responsible for some crime, which you are to deter-mine under the testimony in the case. After passing that question, if you should come to the conclusion that he was a responsible being, capable of understanding the nature and quality of his act, and that it was wrong; that he was responsible before the law for some criminal act in de-priving this woman of her life; then you proceed to ex-amine the question, what crime he is guilty of. You will observe from the reading of the statute that this crime, murder in the first degree, must have been committed from a deliberate and premeditated design to effect the death of this person. To constitute it murder in the second degree, it must have been committed with the intent to kill but without premeditation or deliberation. To constitute it manslaughter in the first degree, it must have been committed without any intent to kill, and in the heat of passion.

Now, gentlemen, with these suggestions as to the statutes which govern in this case, I call your attention directly to the testimony which has been given and which bears upon these questions which you are to determine.

First, however, I will call your attention to the statute which provides, that no act committed by a person while in a state of voluntary intoxication shall be deemed less criminal by reason of his having been in such condition. But whenever the actual existence of any particular purpose, motive or intent is a necessary element to constitute a particular species or degree of crime, the jury may take into consideration the fact that the accused was intoxicated at the time, in determining the purpose, motive or intent, with which he committed the act.

Gentlemen, the first witness called was William J. White, who made this map. He explained the location of this house and the location and situation of the rooms and of the different articles of furniture in the house. I call your attention now to his description of what he observed when he went to the house; your attention is called to all of this evidence for the purpose of enabling you to follow it afresh, and for the purpose of gathering from the testimony, from the acts of this defendant, so far as they are disclosed by the testimony, and so far as you are able to do, the operations of this man's mind during that time, for the purpose of determining, under this testimony, what was passing in his mind; what were his motives and what were his intentions; what was actuating him to do or not to do any particular thing on that day; what was prompting him to make any declaration made that day; what was prompting him to withhold an answer to any question which may have been asked him that day; what was prompting him all the way through, from the time of the commission of this act until a day or two beyond had passed. Your attention is called to this evidence for the purpose of enabling you to follow it through afresh and gather from it, so far as you are able to do in judging of men's motives by their acts, what was passing in this man's mind, and what his condition was at that time.

I do not expect to call your attention to the entire description of the condition of this woman immediately after she received these injuries. The description given by this doctor is about the same as that given by every other witness who was called to speak upon that subject.

I call your attention now to the place in this case where this evidence may be legitimately considered.

LESSON LVI.

COURT PROCEEDINGS—*Continued.*

. As has been before stated, there is no controversy but what the wounds upon this woman's head produced her death. There is no controversy as to the manner in which she received those wounds; that she received them at the hands of this defendant. So far as that part of the case is concerned, all of this testimony might well be dismissed without any further consideration; but in the investigation of this entire matter you are, of course, to avail yourself of every item of evidence which will give you any light upon the real questions which you are to determine.

Gentlemen, upon all these matters which have been submitted to you you are the sole judges of the questions of fact. The Court has called your attention to this evidence, not for the purpose of indicating to you any opinion as to how any question which is submitted to you should be decided. That is altogether your province, to dispose of every question of fact in this case. You are charged with that duty. You are to take the law from the Court, and you are to determine the facts from the evidence. The people, the District Attorney representing the people, is required to satisfy you upon these matters, these facts, which you are called upon to ·find beyond a reasonable doubt. You are to examine all this testimony. You are to weigh it all, every word of testimony in this case which bears upon it in any respect, whether your attention has been called to it by the Court or by the counsel or otherwise. You are to examine all of it, and then if, when you have examined this testimony carefully and candidly, you find your minds in such a condition as, upon any questions here to be decided by you, that you are obliged to say: I am not satisfied; I do not know what the fact is; I am in doubt about it; then there is a reasonable doubt, and the defendant is entitled to the benefit of that doubt. You are to find from this evidence, from the evidence itself, to your satisfaction, beyond such a doubt, upon these different questions which are given you in charge.

Gentlemen, you have listened to this case patiently for a long time. It has been, as before stated, elaborately presented by counsel. The Court has gone over the testimony again, largely in detail, for the purpose of refreshing your minds. You will take this case and examine it with the same care which you have given to the trial. You will, of course, acknowledge and understand the responsibility resting upon you, which will be indicated by your verdict; recognize the fact that it is an important case; important to this defendant; more important to him than any other case which could be presented, for none could be presented which would concern more than his life; important to the people who are presenting this case; important to the community, because, for the protection of the community the criminal law is instituted and must be executed; important in every event. You have been selected and placed upon this jury because you are supposed to be entirely free from any bias; from any notion as to the disposition which ought to be made of this case, and, under your oaths, you are simply to decide it according to the law and to the evidence. You are to deliberate upon it carefully; when you reach a conclusion, you are to voice that by your verdict, deliberately and fearlessly, because with the consequences of this trial, neither this Court nor the jury, nor the counsel engaged here, have anything whatever to do. The consequences must take care of themselves. It is for you simply to declare the fact in this case, under your oaths.

Mr. Sickmon: I ask the Court to charge that the defendant, in order to be convicted of murder in the first degree, must not only have formed the design to kill, but must have premeditated and deliberated upon that design.

The Court: I have so charged.

Mr. Sickmon: I ask the Court to charge that in fixing the grade of crime of which the defendant is charged, the evidence as to his intoxication becomes very important, and must be carefully weighed.

The Court: All the evidence in the case, gentlemen, is to be carefully weighed, but it is not the province of the Court to tell you what is important or otherwise. You are to determine the importance of the testimony.

Mr. Quinby: Just one request, if your Honor please: In determining the question of deliberation and premeditation, the jury may consider, as bearing upon this subject, the fact that a dangerous weapon was used; that the wounds inflicted were several in number, and upon a vital part.

The Court: They are to consider every circumstance in the case, as I have already instructed them.

The jury then retired, in charge of sworn officers.

Proceedings Friday morning, May 10, 1889.

Present: The District Attorney, counsel for the defendant, and the defendant in person.

The jury return into court.

The Clerk called the jury.

The Clerk: Gentlemen of the jury, have you agreed on your verdict?

The Foreman: No, sir; we have not.

The Court: Gentlemen, are you differing upon any question upon which the Court can be of service to you?

The Foreman: Yes, sir; we are.

The Court: Do you desire any instructions?

The Foreman: Yes, sir; we do.

The Court: On what subject?

The Foreman: The jury would like to be instructed in regard to the doctor's evidence, in regard to the boy's testimony on the morning of the tragedy, and in regard to the first and second degree.

The testimony of Richard Collins and Dr. Crothers was read by the stenographer.

The Court then re-addressed the jury.

The Court: Is there anything further, gentlemen?

The Foreman: I think not, if the Court please.

The Court: Well, gentlemen, you may retire.

The jury return again into court at 11.18 o'clock A. M., and say they find the defendant guilty of murder in the first degree, as charged in the indictment.

Day of sentence fixed as Tuesday, May 14, at 9.30 o'clock A. M.

VOCABULARY OF MERCANTILE TERMS.

Ad valorem, according to value.

Administrator, one who manages an intestate estate.

Affidavit, a written declaration made under oath.

Annuity, a fixed annual sum of money payable periodically.

Amanuensis, a person who writes what another dictates; a copyist.

Anonymous (*Anon.*), nameless. Often used in place of an author's signature.

Ante-date, to date beforehand.

Assets, available means for the payment of debts.

Assignee, one to whom an assignment is made.

Attachment, a claim on property legally executed.

Assumpsit, an action to recover damages for a breach or non-performance of a contract or promise.

Bankrupt, one who is hopelessly unable to pay his debts; one who is legally adjudged to be so.

Bill, a detailed statement of goods bought or sold.

Bill of exchange, a foreign order for the payment of money.

Bill of lading, a written account of goods shipped.

Bill of sale, a written contract given by the seller to the buyer of personal property.

Bona fide, in good faith.

Bottomry bond, a mortgage or lien upon a vessel.

Brace, a measure of $\frac{5}{8}$ of a yard.

Broker, a money or stock trader.

Brokerage, a percentage for the purchase and sale of money and stocks.

Bill of particulars, a detailed statement of a plaintiff's cause of action.

Bailee, one to whom goods are delivered in trust.

Catty, a Chinese weight of $1\frac{1}{3}$ pound avoirdupois.

Caveat, a notice filed to prevent the taking out of letters patent.

Clearance, a certificate from a custom-house that a vessel has been cleared.

Commission. a percentage allowed for the sale of goods.

Consignee, one to whom goods or wares are consigned.

Contraband goods, articles prohibited by law to be imported or exported.

Counter-order, a revocation of a former order.

Custom-house, a house where vessels are cleared, and where the duties on goods are paid.

Course of action, right to bring an action.

Cross examination, the questioning of a witness by the opposing party.

Codicil, a supplement to a will.

Covenant, a mutual agreement.

Debenture, a writing acknowledging a debt; a certificate entitling an exporter of imported goods to a drawback of duties paid on their importation.

Defaulter, one who fails to pay, or account for money intrusted to him.

Demurrage, forfeit money for detaining a vessel beyond the time specified in her charter-party.

Discount, a deduction from the stipulated price of goods.

Drawee, the person on whom a bill is drawn.

Duty, a government tax on exported or imported goods.

Direct evidence, evidence which applies directly upon the fact to be proved.

Direct examination, the first examination of a witness.

Dividend, a portion alloted to stockholders in dividing the profits.

Deposition, the giving of testimony in writing.

Endorse, to write one's name on the back of a bill or note.

En route, on the way.

Enfeoff, the instrument or deed by which one is invested with the fee of an estate.

Evidence in chief, evidence taken during the direct examination.

Ex officio, by virtue of his office.

Embezzlement, unlawful appropriation of what is intrusted to one's care.

Executor, one who settles the estate of a testator.

Fac-simile, an exact copy.

Foreclose, to cut off a mortgager from his equity of redemption.

Folio, a sheet of paper once folded; in law a sheet of paper containing a certain number of words, generally 100 words.

Fee simple, an estate held by a person in his own right, and descendible to his heirs.

Grand jury, a jury of not less than 12 persons who examine into accusations against persons charged with crime, and report their findings to the court.

Habeas corpus, a writ inquiring into the cause of a person's imprisonment.

High seas, waters of the ocean which are not within the jurisdiction of any country.

Insolvent, not having money, goods, or estate sufficient to pay all debts.

Inventory, a detailed account of goods or property.

Import, to bring in merchandise from a foreign country.

Indemnity, guarantee against loss.

In loco, in the place of.

Invoice, an itemized list of goods bought or sold.

In toto, altogether.

In transitu, during the transit.

Indenture, a writing containing a contract.

Intestate, dying without having made a will.

Jetson, or jettison, the throwing of goods overboard in time of extreme peril.

Lease, a contract granting possession of property for a stipulated time.

Letter of credit, a letter authorizing one person to receive funds on the credit of another.

Liabilities, debts of an individual or claims against him.
Lien, a legal claim upon land, houses, etc.
Liquidation, the act of adjusting and paying debts.

Maturity, the time when a bill falls due.
Merchandise, the common articles of trade.
Mortgage, the granting of an estate in fee as security for the payment of money.
Mortgagee, the person to whom an estate is mortgaged.
Malfeasance, doing that which one has no right to do.
Monopoly, the sole power of vending goods.

Net proceeds, the remainder after deducting all charges from the amount of gross sales.
Notary, or notary public, a person legally authorized to attest to contracts or writings of any kind.
Nom de plume, an assumed or literary title.
Non compos mentis, not in sound mind.

Oyer and terminer, a court whose duty it is to hear and determine.

Payee, the person to whom money is to be paid.
Per annum, by the year.
Pro forma, according to form.
Parol evidence, oral or verbal evidence.
Post mortem, after death.
Premises, things previously mentioned, houses, lands, etc.
Prima facie, on the first view of the matter.

Quarantine, the detaining of a ship when suspected of contagion.

Resources, money, funds, or that which may be converted into supplies.
Revenue, income ; customs and duties.

Salvage, a reward allowed for saving property from loss at sea.
Sine die, without fixing the day.
Smuggling, passing goods into a country without paying duties.
Stipulation, a contract or agreement.

Tonnage, the capacity of a vessel.

Trustee, a person to whom anything is committed.

Testator, one who makes a will.

Underwriter, one who insures ; an insurer.

Voucher, a paper or document which serves to vouch the truth of accounts.

Verbatim, word for word.

Versus, against ; generally written as an abbreviation, thus : *vs.*

Voire dire, an oath taken by a witness to tell the truth, pronounced vwär deer.

Vend, to sell ; to transfer for a pecuniary consideration.

VOCABULARY OF ABBREVIATIONS AND SIGNS.

@, at; to.

Acct., account.

ⁿ/ₑ, account.

Amt., amount.

Anon., anonymous.

Ans., answer.

Ave., avenue.

A 1, first class.

A. B., bachelor of arts.

Atty., attorney.

Adv., adverb.

Adv., advertisement.

A. D., (*Anno Domini*) ; in the year of our Lord.

A. M., before noon; in the year of the world; master of arts.

Bal., balance.

B. B., bill-book, or bank-book.

Bbl., barrel.

B. C., before Christ.

Bot., bought.

Bu., bushel.

C., cents.

C. B., cash-book.

C. H., court-house.

Co., company.

C., hundred.

Com., Commissioner.

C. O. D., collect on delivery.

Cr., credit or creditor.

Cwt., hundred weight.

D. B., day-book.

Dept., Department.

Dis., discount.

Do, (ditto) the same.

Doz., dozen.

Dr., debtor or doctor.

ds., days.

d., pence.

ea., each.

e. g., for example.

E. E., errors excepted.

Esq., Esquire.

Eng., English.

Ex., example.

et al., and others.

etc., &c. (*et cætera*), and so forth.

Exc., exchange.

Fol., folio.

Ford., forward.

Frt., freight.

Gov., Governor.

G. A., general average.

Gal., gallon.

Gent., gentleman.

Hhd., hogshead.

Hdkfs., handkerchiefs.

Hund., hundred.

I. B., invoice-book.

Id. (*idem*), the same.

i. e. (*id est*), that is.

Inv., invoice.

Ins., insurance.

Ibid., (*ibidem*), in the same place.

Inst., (instant), the present month.

Int., interest.

Invt., inventory.

J. F., journal folio.

lbs., pounds.

Ledg., ledger.

L. F., ledger folio.

L. S., left side (*locus sigilli*), place of the seal.

l., s., d., pounds, shillings, pence,

M., a thousand.

M. C., member of congress.

Mdse., merchandise.

M. D., doctor of medicine.

Mo., month.

Messrs., gentlemen; sirs.

Mme., madame.

MSS., manuscript.

No., or ꝯ number.

N. B., (*Nota Bene*), take notice.

N. P., notary public.

Nov , November.

Oct., October.

O. K., all correct.

Per cent., %, or *per centum*.

Payt., payment.

Par., paragraph.

P. C. B., petty cash-book.

P. M. postmaster.

Pd., paid.

P. O., post-office.

Pkg., package.

pp, pages.

L. & G., loss and gain.

P. S., postscript; written after.

pr, *per;* by.

Pub., publisher.

Prox. *(proximo)*, the next month.

Qr., quarter; quire.

Ques., question.

q. v. (*quod vide*), which see.

Recd., received.

Rev., reverend.

R. R., rail road.

S. B., sales-book.

Secy., or Sec., secretary.

Sept., September.

Sec., second.

S. S., Sunday-school.

ss. (*scilicet*), namely.

Supt , superintendent.

Ult. (*ultimo*), last month.

U. S. A., United States of America; United States Army.

U. S. M., United States Mail.

U. S. N., United States Navy.

viz., to wit; namely.

Vol., volume.

V. P., vice-president.

vs. (*versus*), against.

wk., week.

yds., yards.

yr., year.